The book is dedicated to my parents, Wing Commander (late) Anthony Michael Furtado and Marie Loretta Romana Pereira Furtado.

About the Author

Marianne de Nazareth is presently a full-time freelance journalist writing on a variety of environmental and gender issues. She has won the Laadli Media award for Print Journalism for Gender Sensitivity 2016. In December 2015, she won the best Print Journalism award for Environmental writing and received a cheque for Rs. 50 thousand from the German government.

In 2004, she joined the Deccan Herald as Chief Sub Editor and went on in 2006 to do a Masters in Journalism (Erasmus Mundus Masters in Journalism) funded by the EU to upgrade her journalism skills. She attended three Universities throughout the course - Denmark, Amsterdam and Wales, UK. which was an intensive, full time course for two years, from 2004 - 2006.

She came back to the Deccan Herald in 2008 and worked as Assistant Editor handling the Edit and the Op-Ed pages till 2011.

From 2011, Marianne has been adjunct faculty at St. Joseph's PG College of Media Studies. She has written several papers in the course of her PhD studies and has just submitted her doctoral thesis to the Madurai University entitled Man vs. Elephant Conflict: A Case Study on Print Media Framing of Public Discourse.

She is also a media fellow with the UNFCCC, UNEP & the Robert Bosch Stiftung and travels covering Gender, Science and Environment issues.

Writing still continues to be her first love but her focus has changed to Environmental and Science Journalism with a strong focus on conservation, species loss and gender issues. She writes for a host of Indian and International publications, and is invited to attend Science Conferences to be educated on various issues of sustainability on the planet.

Marianne has written a children's book of stories called 'The One Eyed Ogre & Other stories' and a novel published by Leadstart Publishing called 'Above the Rice-fields of Pilerne.'

She lives in Bangalore with her youngest son, Steven and her husband, Gregory. And spends the rest of her free time visiting her older sons in Woking, UK (David) and Knoxville, Tennessee (Andrew).

Acknowledgements

To,

My parents, who instilled the joy of reading in me since childhood with the gift of books for Christmas, rather than toys.

Malini Nair, my editor, who immediately responded positively to my manuscript saying, "I am aware that you published *Above the Rice fields of Pilerne* with us; it is a wonderful book." Thank you for believing in me.

The Erasmus Mundus Masters in Journalism of which I was a Fellow, doing my Masters in Journalism, from 2006 to 2008 starting in the beautiful Aarhus, Denmark, going on to cosmopolitan Amsterdam and finishing in picturesque Swansea in Wales. This Masters opened up my mind to research and instilled in me that anything I wrote to be published, had to be grounded in solid peer reviewed research.

The UNFCCC and UNEP who had faith in my journalistic capacities and invited me as a fellow for all the Climate Change and Species Loss conferences across the world for over a decade. These interactions made me look at the science of life and living with a keener and more logical eye.

The humbling experience of doing a PhD in the Madurai Kamaraj University, where again research was all important as a base for my thesis. And which has helped in my research about the nebulous world of Parkinson's and looking at the disease with less emotion based understanding.

My sons and husband who have felt the pain along with me, of my parents degenerating from the strong and supportive human beings that they were, to the completely dependant shadows of themselves, with the onset of the disease.

And to my sister Christine, who read the first draft of my

manuscript, and who advised and encouraged me along the way.

Thank you!

Marianne Furtado de Nazareth

Contents

The Poinsettias

As one ages, eventually, no matter what regime you've followed, no matter how fiercely you've fought the fight, good health becomes harder to maintain. It may disappear overnight or simply dwindle, but with every year that passes, the odds shorten.

Laurie Graham

The poinsettias blazed a brilliant red and deep pink in the sun, all standing in a row, in the little nursery behind the Hockey Stadium. Sabrina's spirits lifted when she saw them. She asked her husband to park the car closer to the end of the street, away from the nursery, as she believed the prices would go up if they were seen arriving in a car.

"Oh, come on, Sabrina," said her husband in an irritated voice. "You always imagine the prices will be trebled seeing our car. We just have an ordinary i10 and that won't spiral up the prices for heaven's sake."

But Sabrina would have none of it and insisted he park closer to the bus stand. Walking down towards the nursery she looked across the road, through force of habit, at the dentist's clinic. Her dentist, whom she was visiting more often than she liked, as her teeth were breaking down.

She had "lost" five teeth in the dentist's clinic the previous week and she shuddered as she thought of the implants that were going to be fixed into her mouth. "Oh, stop it," she told herself as she walked forward, deftly dodging a motorbike and an auto-rickshaw who almost drove straight into her. "Think of happier things, and forget the inevitable," she thought as she stood in front of the little nursery filled with newer plants, all brought in for the season.

The poinsettias looked better up close and Sabrina immediately decided she wanted two of them. Bending down she selected the ones she wanted to take home while bargaining for a good price. "Rs. 300 each," said the man in charge. "Two for Rs. 500," she replied and struck a bargain. 'The traders and small businessmen must have been hit hard by the recent demonetization that has been announced,' she thought, when the man accepted the price without any argument. Normally he would not back down so easily.

Then her eyes were drawn to the pretty and always flowering bougainvillea and she decided to purchase four of those as well. Four people hovered around, the man's wife and in-laws it seemed, while the bargain was struck. Obviously the sales proceeds hinged on the food they would get to eat for the day. For the first time Sabrina realised that the family seemed keen on a sale.

Once cash exchanged hands - precious notes which take hours to collect from the bank - the plants were carried towards the car parked a short distance away. Not willing to take any chances, the poinsettias were loaded into the front of the car, near her feet and then they were off, headed to the supermarket to collect groceries. Holding the pots between her feet kept them stable, and prevented them from tipping over and the flowers from snapping off.

Sabrina liked the new supermarket because they were able to get change for the crazy pink Rs. 2000 note which was released by the government in lieu of the Rs. 1000 and Rs. 500 notes in circulation. More often than not, they were stuck with no change if they went to a bakery and tried to buy a loaf of bread with the Rs. 2000 note. "No change, Madam," they were told shortly, so either they signed up for an IOU if the trader so accepted or they left without purchasing anything. It was the downside of demonetization, which seemed to be the bane of the moment. Once more notes started flowing into the market, they were sure the glitches would be cleared. But it was taking a long time for the flow to actualize and open up the squeeze in the market.

Taking the plants home, Sabrina placed the deep pink poinsettias against the black decorative terracotta piece she was so proud of in the balcony. Standing back, she thought, 'Ah, the colour blends in so well with the black. It feels like Christmas now and its sad Mum can't really see them.'

Sabrina's mother suffered from Parkinson's and sadly the beginnings of Alzheimer's, and except for the odd smile of recognition once in a while, she sat quietly in her wheelchair all day, just staring vacantly around the room.

Sabrina inherited her love for plants from her parents and she was sad to see her mother in such a depressingly vegetative state. It gave her nightmares sometimes, worrying if she was headed for the same doom.

"Mum, see the new poinsettias I have brought home

for Christmas!" said Sabrina cheerfully, wheeling her Mum towards the plants.

Her Mum just hung her head downwards, quiet and still. No response.

"Mum, Mum, see the flowers!" said Hema, her help, trying her luck with energising Mum to respond.

"Look, it's a new colour, a deep *mithai* pink rather than the regular red, Mum," said Sabrina.

She brought the plant up close to her mum's face, but Sabrina's mum did not respond and the tears flowed unchecked from Sabrina's eyes, coupled with sobs of despair, as she watched her.

When Alzheimer's strikes, it not only takes the patient's short term memory, but destroys the joy and peace of a family. Wiping her tears away, Sabrina remembered the days she spent in the very same garden, helping Mum and Dad clear some pots, or pick some *chickoos* or custard apples off the trees. Her mother standing in the garden at night, pointing out the constellations of stars to her as a child and then later to her sons.

Her mother bringing in the pot of the exotic Flower of Bethlehem which flowers only after dark. Her excited invitation to all the neighbours, to view the spectacle over a hot cup of coffee and cookies. And then the elation of the breathtaking flower, being shared with her immediate community.

These were parents full of life and love, reduced to a shadow of themselves by the dreaded combination of Parkinson's and Alzheimer's. It's rare for both parents to get Parkinson's, their doctor had explained. But her Dad's contracting the disease was due to the side effects of some other medication. Sabrina's mother was the bona fide Parkinson's, which came on in her 70s. Watching her parents deteriorate before her very eyes was slow torture for Sabrina and her only sibling Samara.

Perhaps this book will bring some solace to others, who have parents afflicted by the dreaded disease, of which there is no cure to date.

New Learnings

Sabrina and Samara were sisters brought up by parents who were go-getters and champions. A father who represented Mysore State in Athletics and Hockey as a young student engineer and a mother who did her Masters in Literature when she had reached the ripe "old" age of 50.

They were the epitome of what a balanced parent should be, even down to helping their daughters with their kids, when they had them, and needed the support.

As kids the parents were out on the playing field with them, encouraging them to excel in their chosen sports. Their homework was supervised by their mother, a teacher, who was keen to see them score well in all subjects, including the second language. Her parents' lives centred around their kids, but they also found time to go out together, not just for the formal parties, but for a movie whenever a new one came to town.

"Let them learn how to speak Hindi," said Sabrina's Dad. "There is no need to make them learn English first, they will learn that from us anyway." And so the girls learned Hindi from the domestic help before they learned how to speak English, which stood them in good stead, as they grew up in Delhi. Learning the language made a huge difference to their lives, as they were included in group activities with their peers in school, rather than overlooked as English-speaking kids.

"Oh, you're Anglo-Indian," was a stereotype they could do without, as their roots were in Goa and they were totally Indian. Having travelled so much they did not speak either Portuguese or Konkani, as their grandparents and parents had settled in various parts of India and Africa so they were more accustomed to Gujarati and Portuguese with a smattering of Konkani. The girls, however, were fluent in Hindi, which helped them gel with their classmates while in Delhi and when the shift to Bangalore occurred, they quickly assimilated and spoke Tamil with the domestic help and Kannada in offices and banks. It was not easy to pick up, but again they knew if they did not shape up, they would be left out.

"It makes me mad when Indira speaks in Tamil to the vendors," said Sabrina with irritation about her house help. "I need to learn as she seems to understand English of late!"

Over a couple of years, forcing herself to speak regardless of the crazy laughs her anglicised Tamil drew, Sabrina learned to speak Tamil which could be understood by Indira. Slowly, she realised that even though the servants shouted when they spoke to one another in the South, they were not fighting. It was just their tone of voice.

Sabrina's Dad, having grown up in the South, in Bangalore and Chennai, knew all the festivals and traditions of the South and she never forgot, when she came of age at twelve years old, what her Dad had said to her. "In the South, they spend a lot of money having wonderful feasts and functions when a girl comes of age. The girl has a coming-of-age ceremony, is dressed in bridal finery, sits on a special throne-like seat and is feted. Instead you are crying because you can't participate in the long jump finals in school. Stop crying and go out there and participate like all the others."

Sabrina, who had been crying and whining that morning, decided to heed her father's instructions and went off to participate in the selections. Bending down to take off at the end of the run up to the pit, she let her father's words echo through her mind, "In the South, girls are feted," and she put all her energy into the jump, clearing more than any of the other girls. After that, whenever that time of the month came around it never bothered her, and her lady coach in school explained that exercise helped in curbing any sort of cramps she would get through the week. There was never a question of non-participation in sports after that.

Music was another skill where the girls were encouraged mainly by their Dad. They attended pianoforte classes in school and sat for all the Trinity College of Music exams. In those days, the examiners came from London and the girls were always dressed in almost identical home-made frocks, on the practical exam day.

"I have embroidered your blouses differently, if that helps," said their Mum most matter-of-factly, as they disliked being dressed similarly. It was with great relief that their mother stopped dressing them alike when they turned teenagers. Everywhere they went people admired their beautiful outfits and remarked on how talented their mother was as a seamstress. Neither girl could stitch like their mother and in any case 'ready-made' was all the rage, when they had their families.

"You have practised every morning, all through the year," said their father, "And your Mum has made the most beautiful dresses, specially for your exam and you have new matching shoes too. Go for the exam with confidence and play your best. Don't let nervousness spoil all the work you have put in throughout the whole year." And that gave them the confidence to go calmly into the exam and always pass with Honours and high accolades. Just those few words, changed the manner in which the girls viewed anything they handled in their lives after that.

It was not that their mother was quiet, but she supported their Dad in all his decisions and stepped in when he went over the top with discipline. Both parents spent all their free time with the family and it was only when they had their own families, that the girls realised how giving with their time their parents had been.

Who would have expected the dreaded disease called Parkinson's to hit them one after the other and reduce these two solid individuals who never had "can't" in their vocabulary, to slowly degenerate into helpless vegetables? From feeding them to changing them, they needed help with everything. The family was suddenly faced with a bend in the river of their lives. A bend which would never revert to flowing smoothly and unwaveringly again.

As the disease progressed, Sabrina's parents needed support with lots of everyday activities like eating and drinking, standing up and moving about, getting dressed and washing. They found it increasingly difficult to move, and according to research, some people can only speak very quietly or not at all. They even have trouble with swallowing water, which is the condition Sabrina's mother was finally reduced to.

This book hopes to help people come to terms with this disease which currently has no cure. But helps the carer understand that it's a long haul forward, with no end really in sight, of any sort of recovery. The book makes the reader understand that enjoying the beauty of a parent in one's life is the focus—because one is never prepared for the silent killer that strikes and reduces them to frail shells of themselves.

Full Of Life

Sabrina reminisced about the birthday celebration parties that were held for them as kids. Her mum was in her element then with her skill at making delicious snacks. Tables groaning with goodies—pin wheel sandwiches, cakes made in the house; *pakoras* and coconut pancakes, bright pink and white coconut *burfi* and savoury boats filled with a succulent sardine fish & onion mix. But best of all were the lemon tarts, coconut cones and peanut brittle. All made from scratch and not a thing bought from the shops, all made with top-of-the-line ingredients.

There was a special table cloth with Disney characters used for the kiddy parties and glossy, shiny ones for the adult parties. And of course the flowery, English curtains that were folded away all year, and smelled of moth-balls. The girls never needed to help as Sabrina's Dad always had everything under control. Mum and Dad made a fantastic team, whether it was getting everything organised or clearing up after the party. They worked together, ensuring a good time was had by all, including themselves.

"Can you help to fill the coconut cones, Sabrina?" asked Mum at one party when she had turned twelve. The coconut had been scraped by Parvati, the cook, and Mum had stirred and mixed the *elaichi*, sesame seeds, plums and sugar into the mix, on a low flame, letting the mass become slightly gooey, before the bright pink cochineal was added. Mum never minded if she popped a spoon or two of the mix into her mouth, as she helped.

"Just see that there is enough to fill all the cones, and push the mix down or people will waste half the cone," said Mum. Making the cones was a lot of work with the strips of pastry rolled out and wound dexterously around the outside of the steel cone shape, fixing down the end by pressing it firmly. The cones and other bases were made by Mum over the week and stored in airtight containers.

The cones were then placed in a *kadai* of boiling oil and in minutes the cone slipped off and the steel form was taken out with a fork. The cones were then left to cool and then stored in an airtight tin. In those days they used tins, no Tupperware. Old biscuit tins were favourites and kept fried food, really crisp.

"Fill the platter up," her mother would say. "Load the cones one against the other, with their pink mouths on the top," and Sabrina and Samara made at least two large platters of them.

Her mother's *chutney* sandwiches were legendary, and she had friends who said they came to enjoy only those. In fact, one of her friends made a meal of only the *chutney* sandwiches. That was disgusting but he did, and Sabrina and Samara were told to keep quiet because the man was their father's boss.

The *chutney* was made with only the freshest coriander leaves, which were picked and the tender shoots on top of each stalk. A bunch of mint leaves and a ball of softened tamarind with a couple of de-seeded dates, were added. Half a scraped fresh coconut and Parvati sat down at the grinding stone with a steel plate full of ingredients to grind. She began rolling the grinding stone and pushing and rolling and pushing the mix into the grinding cup. "A few sprigs of tender curry leaves from the top of the tree," Sabrina's Mum would call out and the kids went sprinting to the curry leaf tree in the garden, to add to the fragrant mix, as Parvati ground, making a perfect *chutney*.

"Watch how to make it perfect," said her Mum as if she was letting her into a huge secret. Cutting big slices of Amul butter, she added it into the deep green *chutney* and finally a small sprinkle of salt and a generous squeeze of fresh lime was added, carefully taking out the seeds.

"You don't want to make your *chutney* bitter," her Mum would advise and they hastily picked out any stray lemon seeds, laughing while doing it. The butter helped to smooth the *chutney* onto the freshly sliced bread, and also made the sandwiches extra delicious with every bite.

"Only the freshest of bread, for the best of *chutney* sandwiches," intoned her Mum and Sabrina took the tradition to her home, where day old bread is made into toast in the house, not sandwiches.

The lemon tart cases too were baked in advance and cooled and stored into biscuit tins. Making the pastry from scratch was another one of Sabrina's Mum's fortes. She always told them to leave the pastry to "rest" after pounding it, as then it would be easier to roll out. To make the pastry, they mixed the flour into softened butter to produce a smooth dough. They then, took a large bit of the pastry and rolled it out and cut it with a steel glass. They pressed the dough into small 3 inch tart pans and refrigerated the crust for 30 minutes, after pricking the base of each with a fork.

"Always preheat the oven to 350 °F and bake the crusts until light golden brown, for 15 to 20 minutes," said their Mum. Sabrina swore that she had never tasted tarts like her Mum's anywhere else in the world. This was because making the filling of each tart, she stood and thickened it all herself, making sure the lemon curd never curdled and remained at dropping consistency.

"Spoon the lemon curd into the tart with a tablespoon, after putting the tart cases out on a platter," and those lemon tarts added zest and zing to the table. Everything was done so effortlessly and happily and many years later Sabrina did the same for her kids' parties. Nothing was bought, everything was home-made, including the vadas and the cake which was always made in the shape, the birthday girl requested.

Ladybugs and cars, cricket pitches and aeroplanes, a large single football and even a swimming pool with marzipan figures swimming across or Barbie doll dress cakes. Her mum taught her to be adventurous and she felt that she enjoyed her kids parties, 'cause she enjoyed her own too.

As she sipped her tea, her eyes moist while reminiscing, Sabrina's mind went back to her mother's halcyon days. The life and soul of the party in her very dressy sarees and high heels. Where had she gone? Where was that mother who could fill a table groaning with party snacks? The doctor had told her that she could recover at first, so they spent time talking to her, but most days now she did not recognise the family. Sabrina watched as she lived in a sort of limbo, with a smile of recognition sometimes on hearing a familiar voice, but most times a blank look, with a mouth working hard, trying to say something that won't come out.

Parkinson's is a disease marked by muscle tremors, muscle rigidity, decreased mobility, stooped posture, slow voluntary movements, and a mask-like facial expression. Sabrina began to research Parkinson's on the online U.S. National Library of Medicine (NLM) website which has millions of books and journals about all aspects of medicine and health care on its shelves. The NLM was founded in 1836 and is part of the National Institutes of Health (NIH) in Bethesda, Maryland.

Parkinson's is a disease of the nervous system that mostly affects older people. It typically begins after the age of 50. The disease can be very hard to live with because it severely restricts mobility and as a result makes daily activities increasingly difficult.

Parkinson's is also a progressive disease, which means that in most cases it will continue to gradually get worse. Many people who develop Parkinson's will require full time nursing care. It is incurable and its exact cause is not known, but there are effective medication and treatments available that can relieve its symptoms slightly.

Unconventional Dreams

"I want to do my Masters, it will make a difference to my teaching and how people view me in school," announced Sabrina's mother one day. She was well into her 50s then and clearly did not look it, or feel it.

"I will check with the Bangalore University if they have an external degree which you can do by correspondence," said Dad.

She had no computer or Google to help research back then and had to physically go to libraries to be able to research all that was in the curriculum. It was hard bringing up the girls who were at varying stages of growth and do her Masters simultaneously, but she never let hard work faze her. Today's researchers have the wonderful support of Google where everything is at your finger tips. One can sit and work on an entire thesis from a single laptop and scan the world wide web for International Journals to support one's analysis. Sabrina's mother had no such luck and had to physically read through books, which she had to scour libraries in the city for.

"There are some books in the British Council Library, according to one of the teachers in school. So, let me just become a member at the library and check out the books there," said her mother, pulling on her walking shoes to walk up to the library.

After that she spent long hours in the Literature section of the library which was just above Koshy's, a well-known bakery and restaurant in Bangalore. Interestingly, her Dad helped too and the girls found it enjoyable to see them make a team effort of her Masters. Books used to be spread out over the dining table and copious notes were taken manually from books, which their Dad very seriously walked to the British Library to exchange or search for.

Their mother loved learning about the different streams of Literature and was keen on the American Literature module, to pursue a course of study focusing on American literary texts and other cultural literary aspects. Obviously not much of American Literature was available in the British Library and so Sabrina's parents contacted the USIS in New Delhi and Samara borrowed novels and poetry anthologies from the US Consular library in Chennai for her Mum to help her study that module.

The selection of literature she was given to read through included *Moby Dick* and *The Adventures of Huckleberry Finn* by Mark Twain. Sabrina's Mum's favourite American writer was John Steinbeck and his *Grapes of Wrath*. Her mother swore the book ripped her nerves to rags, as the novel was about a poor family, driven from their land during the Great Depression. It was the main reason Steinbeck was awarded the 1962 Nobel Prize for Literature, she said trying to persuade Sabrina to read her copy.

Of course, Sabrina started reading in real earnest only once her kids grew older and she had more time on her hands. Then she enjoyed the American classic by JD Salinger—*The Catcher in the Rye.*

With India's legacy of British Literature, Sabrina's

mother enrolled in the British Literature module too, to indulge in a course of study focusing on British literary texts and of course their poetry anthologies that she had loved since her youth.

She deepened her understanding of both the role of narrative and literary form of British literature. Like the American module, the literature was analysed with regard to shaping the experiences and articulating the philosophical, political and social questions central to British history and culture. This module had a surfeit of texts which they rented from the British Library and spent hours wading through. From Charles Dickens, Jane Austen, Virginia Woolf, the suddenly iconic Lewis Carroll, Emily Bronte, Somerset Maugham and the wildly erotic D.H. Lawrence. Their mother was never too fond of the more modern writers like Roald Dahl, Doris Lessing, Salman Rushdie and Julian Barnes. But she did enjoy Rudyard Kipling and she encouraged Sabrina and Samara to read all of Enid Blyton's series through their formative years.

One author Sabrina was crazy about and wanted all books to read of, at once, was Rumer Godden. The author spent an idyllic childhood on a tributary of the Brahmaputra, in North India and her novels had a timeless shimmer, with very adult themes. Her characters were from the pre-partition British India and the Indians they governed and a lot was about a small town named Narayanganj in West Bengal. The best of Godden's books according to Sabrina were "*Greengage Summer*" and "*Kingfishers on Fire*". In fact from the book *Kingfishers on Fire*, Sabrina decided to call the cottage she built in Bangalore—*Dilkhush*, after the house in the book.

Comparative and World Literature was another module which interested both Sabrina's parents where they were to pursue a broadly interdisciplinary course of study, focusing on the comparative analysis of literary texts and other cultural traditions, this time from across the globe. Having travelled widely both parents were keen to deepen their knowledge of the history of literary and narrative forms across a broad range of national literatures, cultures and historical periods, as well as exploring the complex relationship of literary works from politics, philosophy and the visual arts. The beauty of cultures were echoed in various literature and gave them great insights into how the littérateurs of the world plumbed their cultures, to give a different flavour and style to their writing.

And then the final module chosen was Film, Literature, and Visual Culture. Sabrina's mum and dad were rabid film buffs and went for every film that came to town. They were all set to pursue a broadly interdisciplinary course of study focusing on the comparative analysis of film in its relationship to literature, as well as other visual media, across a large range of national cultures and aesthetic traditions.

It was interesting for the girls to see them read a piece of literature and then watch the film, deepening their ability to interpret films and other works. Not only was this in the light of the cultural and social conditions of their production, but also in their relationship to the history of literary genres and aesthetic forms. They watched the films on videos hired from the local video library, and had long, heated discussions over cups of tea about them.

There was no more sitting around, waiting for children or grandchildren to arrive to spice up their lives at home. Sabrina and Samara found that their academics kept them very busy and happy for two whole years. They re-read Jane Austen's 'Pride and Prejudice' and then sat back with coffee and bondas to watch the film and then write a comparative essay assignment on the film and the book. In fact, they were hooked onto watching all the various films made on the novel over various decades and decided they enjoyed the 50s era film version, the best.

It was a stupefying two years, watching them work together and frankly Sabrina felt her father should have been awarded the degree as well. Their actual connection on so many different levels made the family realise that they had developed a staggering connection between them in spite of their marriage being arranged, between their families living in Bangalore and Bombay.

Sadly an unfortunate accident with a bus, put paid to Sabrina's mother's dreams, of rising in the school arena and she resigned from school, when she found out that her accident-leg, was not healing as well as it should. However, no one could take from her the joy of being conferred her Masters and the fun she had working towards the degree when she was well into her 50s.

"It was definitely the reason why I did not falter taking on a fellowship in Europe when in my 50s," felt Sabrina and then later Gino, Sabrina's son went back to his books, which he gave up much earlier than he should have, saying, "If my old lady could do a second Masters in her 50s, well I can get back to doing an MBA in my 30s." And he did.

Steady Hands

When Sabrina and Samara were kids, holidays across the North East of India in their Standard Herald were frequent and often. Dad made wonderful holiday plans with Mum and they all piled into the car and drove huge distances as a family. They were based in Shillong and made forays to Darjeeling, Kurseong even as far as Gangtok in Bhutan as her Dad loved the mountains.

They never stayed in expensive hotels, but instead, their Dad booked the Government Dak Bungalow, which was often not spick and span, but the food offered was the old-fashioned British stews and curries, which they all enjoyed. Old musty furnishings hung on the walls and the rooms had huge cavernous cupboards, with enormous king-sized beds.

The back seat of the car was loaded with quilts and pillows just in case they needed them if the rooms were cold. But, most often there was always a fire place in which a fire roared, and they sat around warming their chilled hands. They also enjoyed falling asleep, with the still-crackling bits of wood, snapping in the grate, around the still-smoking cinders.

The Dak bungalow in Darjeeling was an old British style

bungalow, with a rambling garden and a corrugated tin roof painted green. All around the bungalow were manicured lawns and flower beds in which grew a profusion of roses and chrysanthemums. The rust coloured chrysanthemums stood out with their raggedy petals, but the pots of single white or yellow chrysanthemums were the prize winners of the garden. Each plant was adorned with just one chrysanthemum which was supported on a neat, slim bamboo support. A wall of delicately scented sweet peas stood on one side of the garden, where a riot of different coloured sweet peas grew and were supported, on a neat bamboo trellis.

Red, pink, maroon, purple and a brilliant white rainbow of sweet peas, crept up the trellis their sweet perfume filling the entire garden. "I use only *gobra*, a mixture of cow-dung and other wet waste that I make in the compost pit near the kitchen. All the wet waste of the Dak Bungalow, from the kitchens, is thrown into the pit everyday and the constant rain breaks it down. I don't use any chemicals," shared the *maali* very happily with their Dad as he walked around showing off his babies.

"Here are a few mixed seeds of the sweet peas which will grow well in Shillong," said the *maali* handing over a packet of seeds to their Dad who was delighted to receive them as he was a garden person too. The girls heard him excitedly giving the packet to their Mum, to keep safely and he promised to make a wall of sweet peas when winter came around in Shillong. "Just let me check how he makes the trellis," said their Dad, all his engineering skills coming to the fore. He was also promised a clump of rust coloured chrysanthemum plants, just before they left for home.

"Once the flowers are cut back there are a number of new little runners which grow at the base of the mother plant which can be split up and are perfect for propagation. We don't buy plants from any nursery, we grow them all ourselves, either from seed or from seedlings and runners," said the *maali* with pride in his voice, as he showed the family around his lush garden.

"Did you know the chrysanthemum is a symbol of the Emperor and the Imperial family in Japan?" Dad asked the girls. They shook their heads, storing away the new piece of general knowledge.

"Remember my silk house coat and the Japanese umbrella that Uncle Edward gave me after his return from Japan? They are both ornamented with gold silky chrysanthemums and the stunning red crowned cranes," explained Mum. "Remind me to show it to you once we return to Shillong."

Sabrina and Samara ran around the garden collecting pine cones in a bag, which they planned to take home and use as Christmas decoration. There were hundreds of pine cones all over the extensive lawns, so the girls began to pick and choose the best ones they wanted to keep. The rest fed the fire in their room.

"Ask the orderly if you can throw the extra cones into the fire he sets up this evening," suggested Mum. The girls were most excited about that and went out with renewed vigour, collecting more.

At the time Sabrina and Samara's parents were probably in their early 40s and were fit and strong. The little fountain in the centre of the garden stood in a pond filled with deep royal purple Water Lilies.

"I am sure there are gold fishes in the pond," said their Dad, "let's go and check them out."

Squealing with excitement and delight, the girls stared entranced at the arresting purple lilies, dew drops glinting on them in the morning sun. Below the flowers swam large, plump gold fish, flashing in and out of the plate shaped lotus leaves, floating on the water. They were thrilled to watch their Dad try to scoop up one fish out for them, with an oversized tea strainer and put it into a jar so they could enjoy it for their stay. His hand was strong, and his fingers nimble and adroit as he scooped a second fish with one fluid movement, and deposited it into the bottle too. Dad had tough sinewy hands, which he used constantly to repair things or work with. He was a hands-on Dad, always helping them with their art or science projects.

"Everyone, it's time for lunch, you can go back to play later," called their Mum. She was impeccably dressed in a Tussar silk saree which she had bought in Shillong. Being a service officer's wife she was always dressed in sarees and her collection were mainly silk, which she or their Dad purchased periodically.

Their mother was always carefully dressed and every pleat of her saree was knife-edged and flawless, neatly in place. The girls loved watching her sit at the dressing table and flip her hair into a French chignon with consummate ease. Her fingers adroitly pushing pins in, to hold her hair in place. The girls curiously watched her do her hair, as she had a thick head of shiny black hair and never kept it too long, so she could maintain it well.

Her fingers were slim and long and Sabrina was very pleased, when many years later, her mother's sister grabbed her hands in far away Germany, chortling with delight and saying with much excitement, "You have our fingers, you have our fingers!"

Those same slim fingers quiver uncontrollably now, in fact her whole hand too, if she tries to pick up anything and she is unable to do anything for herself, bathe, feed or dress and needs help 24x7 for everything. Parkinson's, the silent killer, quietly crept in and ruined her quality of life forever. Because of her old age and the onset of Diabetes she was unable to have any of the invasive treatments, to improve her quality of life.

A Firm Hold

The girls never forgot their wonderful holidays in Baroda with their maternal grandparents. It did not matter where Sabrina or Samara were, the family went down to Baroda for a whole month during their summer vacations. It was not easy, but the family was booked into a First Class train compartment, well in advance and travelled for at least two days to their destination. In those days air travel was not undertaken by the common man and most often was reserved, mainly for the rich, as it was very expensive.

"Go and look, our names will be listed on the reservation chart put up on each bogie," said their Dad. Excitedly, the girls ran to search the charts for their names and laughed at the strange and incorrect spelling of their names.

"Look, look! Mine is Satrinu and yours is Semaru and we have got a coupé," said the girls animated at the prospect, of having a compartment all to themselves.

They rushed to find their parents to give them the news. "Dad, Dad! Come see our names on a coupé, but they are spelled wrong," they said excitedly. "At least I think they are ours, as they begin with an S. The spellings are completely wrong, though."

Grabbing hold of the girls' hands, their Dad walked quickly and firmly towards the chart, with the girls bouncing up and down alongside him. There was a large crowd peering at the chart so he walked up to the conductor instead, who was strolling past and asked to check his chart.

"Are my daughters names on the list please, Sir? Samara and Sabrina?" he asked.

The conductor, all spiffy in his white uniform and peaked cap, ran his finger down the list searching for the names and just like the girls had said, came upon the wrongly spelled names.

"Yes! Here are the names," he said tapping on the chart with his pen, with the booked coupé details, to the excited squeals of the girls.

"I thought you were old enough to travel in your own compartment and act responsibly," said their Dad to the girls high-spirited and exuberant responses, when they realised they were going to be given their own compartment.

"Of course we can be on our own, and look after one another," said Sabrina, while they checked out the appealingly compact coupé, with it's twin berths and mini table on which they could place their water and food.

"Come, help me carry your suitcases in," said their Dad, while they jumped up and ran along the passageway in the bogie, looking for their Mum who was standing with the luggage on the platform with the coolie.

Dad hoisted the large trunks, onto the rolled cloth the coolie had placed on his head, with ease. His hands were strong and broad with a gold ring that flashed on the fourth finger and there was nothing that he found too heavy to carry. The trunks were going into their coupé, while the lighter suitcases, he went back for, were pushed under the seats in the girls coupé.

The whistle blew and the guard waved his green flag, while the girls sat quietly with thrilled expressions in their coupé. As the train pulled out of the station, it belched out a huge cloud of black smoke, from the engine.

Sabrina leaned her face against the bars of the window, trying to look out at the powerful chugging engine and the clattering bogies behind. Clack, clack went the bogies on the rails beneath, as the huge wide expanses of fields of sugar-cane flashed by. Specks of coal flew into Sabrina's eyes but she just washed them out with drinking water and enjoyed the acrid smell of the plumes of black smoke flying to her face. Travelling by train has a charm of its own which today's rapid plane travel is devoid off. A train journey was leisurely and more slow-paced when compared to the high speed, instantaneous flights of today with far less joy in the rushed cab rides to the airport, the terrible traffic jams, to finally sit in a crowded plane from whose windows nothing but clouds can be seen.

Their Dad appeared at stations in-between, flashing bottles of cold Fanta in their iconic glass ridged bottles and boxes of cheese sandwiches with boiled eggs, which their Mum always prepared for the journey.

"See, your favourite Fantas," said their Dad, thrusting ice-cold, sweating bottles of Fanta into their eager hands. They all sat down comfortably and opened out the boxes to share. "Take an egg each, peel it and put the shells into the box," instructed Dad. "Pass that salt shaker to me please," he asked, which Sabrina leaned across and gave it to him.

"Pull down the shutters," said Samara, "'Cause all the smoke and dust will fly onto the food."

"Enjoy the food, I am going back to check on your Mum," said Dad, leaving the girls to wolf down their boiled eggs and sandwiches and of course, the delicious ice-cold Fanta.

Arriving in the Vadodara Junction, their father in his typical well-organised fashion asked them to stay put, while their Mum stood while the bigger luggage was unloaded, after which the girls' lighter suitcases were lifted down from the train onto the platform by the coolies.

"Sabrina you hold my hand and walk with me and Samara you hold Mum's hand and we will all follow the coolie," their Dad instructed.

Off the girls went with the two coolies precariously juggling the trunks and the suitcases, while the girls were being firmly held by their parents. In and out and in and out the coolies went, weaving through the huge crowds on the platform, to the Exit gates. The strange smells and sounds were exciting, but their parents kept a firm hold on their hands, as they could get lost in seconds in the milling crowds.

Outside they were guided towards cycle rickshaws who vied with one another to get them into their rickshaw. "Come, Sahib! I will give you a good price. Only Rs. 30 to Fatehgunj."

"Rs. 30 is too much," snapped their Dad and finally they fixed up two rickshaws for Rs. 25 each.

Off they went in the pale dawn of the morning, with large flocks of parrots screeching overhead, heading out from their roosts, to their feeding grounds.

"Look up there, there must be at least 500 birds," said their Dad pointing to a loud screeching cloud in the sky, as the rickshaw lurched forwards.

The sky was streaked with pink and grey, the colours of dawn, with the sun starting to light up the city and wake up the sleeping dogs and children.

"Hold on to the side of the rickshaw so you don't get thrown out as he takes the curve into Fatehgunj," warned their Dad and Samara looked down at his strong square fingers with it's thick gold wedding band on the left hand.

His hands were calloused with all the work he enjoyed doing around the house, repairing things. Hands which the girls grew to depend on to fix everything and anything they wanted around the house, through their growing years. Putting up shelves for their books in their rooms, making an apiary to raise a domestic hive of bees for honey. Even using the shovel expertly to dig out a large hole in which to plant a graft, for their grandfather in the garden.

Soon they reached the old rambling homestead in which their grandparents lived. A large verandah snaked around the frontage and the red paint glowed in the early morning light. The chickens too in the large coop built to one side of the house, had begun industriously clucking and scratching the earth for food. The creeper that hung downwards around the verandah was green and lush and helped keep the verandah cool.

The girls looked excitedly at one another and waved out shouting happily, as they could see their grandparents enthusiastically and eagerly waving back in welcome to them. They were going to be in Baroda for a month and the girls were full of excitement and anticipation.

The Grandparents' House

"Welcome, welcome," said their grandparents amidst hugs and kisses, "How big you have grown!" Their Dad ran back down to the rickshaws and collected the luggage, heaving the suitcases onto the steps coming up into the house. He then went down and paid off the rickshaw men, but there was no way in which he would give them more than the fixed price. Their Dad was stern like a typical service officer, when it came to money and that taught the girls to be frugal and not wasters.

"Twenty-five rupees each. Here is the money," he said thrusting the notes into their hands.

"Give us thirty rupees each instead of twenty-five," demanded the rickshaw men.

"No, we spoke and decided on twenty-five and there's no way I am giving you thirty," said their service-officer dad.

The rickshaw men wiped their faces off sweat, hung their towels on their shoulders and wheeled about, kicking up the dust with their tires and made their way back to the main road.

"Come on girls, let's give your grandparents the special cans of fresh plum jam and pineapple slices that we have brought for them."

Excitedly they opened the trunk which was filled with goodies and gifts for their grandparents. Struggling with the weight of the tins, they managed to pull them out and carry them to the dining table.

"What's in the cans girls?" asked their grandfather with a big smile. "Come see what the girls have brought," he called out to their grandmother.

Looking at the large shiny cans their grandmother went to get the tin opener to open the plum jam. Finally their Dad had to use the strength of his hands to lever the tin opener up and down and open the large can of plum jam.

"Oh my! Come and look at the thick plum jam," and everyone peered into the tin, looking at the delicious looking treacle thick jam, for the first time.

"I need to empty the jam into bottles and keep them in the fridge," said Grandma. "Bring me some of the bottles kept on the lowest shelf in the storeroom please Sabrina."

"They really do a wonderful job at the government factory in Shillong," said their Mum as she helped spoon the jam into the clean and sterilised bottles. "I wonder if we will get other fruit to tin next time like peach halves and even the pears which grow in every garden and which no one bothers to eat as there are so many other varieties of fruit around."

"We kick the wood pears down the hill as we walk back from school," said Samara laughing.

"Yes, the bats eat part of the fruit and drop them, then we get to kick them around as they are as hard as cricket balls," said Sabrina joining in.

"We can save the cans of pineapple slices for the Christmas pineapple trifle," said Grandmother taking the cans away to keep them on the shelf in the storeroom. The storeroom always smelled of fruit and food and especially of the home-made *laddoos* that Grandma made with *til.*

"Sit and eat breakfast girls and then go and have your showers," said their grandmother. "Rosy is making fresh *chappaties* and the fluffy scrambled eggs that you love."

The girls rushed into the kitchen, where on the *tava* Rosy was making the soft and crisp *chappaties* that they enjoyed. Flames licked the sides of the *tava* as the cooking was done on firewood. The *atta* for the *chappaties* was made from freshly ground wheat in the mill close-by. Their grandmother did not believe in ready-made ingredients for anything, including the *masalas* used in the kitchen. Everything was made from scratch and was fresh with no preservatives at all.

"Wash your hands at the tap and come here with plates from the dining room," said Rosy as the girls rushed to get their plates.

"Here Sabrina, a nice big spoon of scrambled eggs and you can eat as many *chappaties* as you like. From today you can take over feeding the hens and collecting the eggs from the hen coop," said Rosy.

The girls settled down to eat on short stools in the kitchen and chatted, telling Rosy about the train journey from Gawahati and all about the coupé and fun they had on their own. Rosy clucked her tongue, when Sabrina polished off her scrambled egg, with just one *chappatie* and told her to go and ask Grandma for a dollop of her mulberry jam to eat her second *chappatie* with.

The girls loved Grandma's mulberry jam, as it was made from the long and luscious mulberries that grew in Grandpa's garden. Only the black and slightly over-ripe ones were picked and literally stewed in sugar and cinnamon. After boiling and simmering on a low flame, the jam would be constantly stirred to prevent it from burning at the bottom. Rosy spread the jam in a thick layer over the whole *chapattie* and then rolled up and they sat happily in the verandah, watching the neighbour's goats eating up the live green-hedge fence between the houses.

"Yuck! Look at their little smelly droppings on the ground," said Samara to Sabrina and they laughed watching the animals.

"Those are called Goat's pills," said Grandma sagely, and the girls have never found out if there is such a word in any language, or if such a word does exist!

"Come with me into the garden with a basket and let's pick *chikoos,"* said their Dad. The girls gobbled up the rest of their *chappaties* and scurried after their Dad into the garden. Their Dad pulled the rickety back gate of the garden open and closed it firmly behind him, in case the goats crept in and ate up the plants.

The *chikoo* tree was towering and immense, spreading its branches across the entire back of the house. There were a whopping number of fruit and all were the oval variety of *chikoo*. Extremely delicious and addictive, especially if they were taken ripe off the tree. The skin of the fruit was remarkably thin and their grandparents just washed and ate them, skin and all.

"You have to be careful that the milk of the fruit does

not fall into your eyes. Just rub it in the mud and that will stop the milk from messing your fingers and the basket," advised their Dad.

By the end of one hour the girls and their father had taken out at least one hundred fruit and it was hard work. Their Dad had agilely perched up in the tree would pick the fruit, put them into a cloth bag attached to a rope and lower the bag for the girls to empty onto the soil.

"We have plenty of *chikoos* to eat while you are here," said Grandma. "Spread them out on newspapers on the floor of the storeroom and come in and eat as many as you like through the day. Now come and have a glass of *nimboo paani* after all that hard work."

Sabrina reminisced about the wonderful holidays they spent as young girls with a strong and healthy father and mother, who taught them all that they knew today as adults. She could see her Dad perched on the tree taking out the fruit and now gone too soon after a debilitating few years where they watched him suffer and die a slow and painful death.

The Chicken Coop

Sabrina and Samara were told nap quietly after lunch every afternoon whilst on holiday in Baroda. They found it difficult at first, just lying there looking out at the Neem trees, which were heavily fruiting. The ripe fruit were eaten by the screeching green, rose- ringed parakeets and mynas and fell off the trees in a mess round the trunk of the tree. The rest made a yellow carpet on the ground, of acrid smelling fruit, with neat oval shaped, white seeds.

"You can take a book off Grandpa's revolving book shelf and go lie down and read," said their Mum while she was able to have some quiet time with Grandma.

The revolving book shelf was an exquisite piece of furniture with carved corners and delicate legs. It was an antique piece, which was the pride and joy of their grandfather. He loved to read only mystery books and had collections of Sherlock Holmes, Agatha Christie, James Hadley Chase and Perry Mason books, which filled the shelves from top to bottom. The girls were free to take any book to read provided they were replaced carefully.

"Do not bend over the edge of the page when you want to mark the spot to where you have read. Instead, use a book mark which will keep the spine of the book strong and not destroy the pages," advised Grandpa. "Here take these book marks and use them in the books while you are here. I want you to read my books, but I don't want them destroyed."

The girls spent long afternoons enjoying his books and did not rest till they read as many as they could during the month they were in Baroda. Sabrina especially loved the Perry Mason books written by Erle Stanley Gardner and never stopped reading till she completed the entire collection that her Grandpa had. *The Case of the Restless Redhead*, *The Case of the Drowning Duck* and *The Case of the Crimson Kiss*, were some of her favourites from the series.

"Do you know the stories were adapted for the TV?" revealed their grandfather, "And 271 different stories were aired and were very popular from the 1950s onwards."

The protagonist of the series was a Raymond Burr, who was a fictional Los Angeles criminal defence lawyer who appeared in all of Gardner's books. Many episodes are based on the novels and short stories written by Gardner, with some stories having been adapted more than once.

One afternoon when the girls were fed up of just lying down, they checked to see what their mother was up to. Both their Grandmum and Mum were in the kitchen making some Guava cheese and the girls knew that would keep them busy for at least an hour.

So they slid out of bed quietly, humping up the pillows like they were asleep and slipped out from the side door to the chicken coop. The chickens were slumbering quietly in the shade of the coop. The summer heat made them pant slightly and their tongues hung out of their beaks.

"Oh look!" said Sabrina. "They look so hungry and tired

and won't lay any eggs for us for breakfast tomorrow."

"Look! You are right, the bowls of food are empty, so let's fill them up with the wheat I have seen Grandpa bring from the garage," said Samara.

"Really? Where? Show me!" said Sabrina, and the girls scuttled quietly towards the garages on the other side of the coop.

"Let's hope the lock on the door is open," said Samara.

"The door makes a very loud squeak as it opens, so we will have to gently and slowly prise it open," warned Sabrina.

The two of them entered the dimly lit, massive garage and Samara pointed to a drum on the side.

"I have seen Grandpa take the wheat in a tin and carry it to the coop to feed the hens," said Samara.

"Okay! I will carry one tin and you can carry the second," said Sabrina in a bossy tone that irritated Samara.

"No! I will carry the first tin, 'cause I showed you what to do," said Samara angrily.

"I am the older one," said Sabrina, "Just wait your turn till I return." And off she went with the first tin to the coop.

Annoyed at having to wait, Samara decided she would just use her palms put together as a scoop and filled them with a heap of wheat and began to walk to the door of the coop too.

Up and down and up and down went the girls for a long time, filling up all the bowls in the large coop. The hens had never seen so much food before and were pecking frantically away while the girls marched up and down from the garage.

"What do you think you are doing?" asked Grandpa in a loud and shocked voice.

The girls had never heard their Grandpa ever raise his voice. He was on his way to the market to buy fruit, with his cloth bag rolled up in his hand, never expecting to see the girls up to such mischief.

Hearing the commotion Grandma and Mum arrived on the scene, clapping their hands to their mouths in horror. A huge trail of wheat lay from the garage to the coop. In their excitement they had over filled the tin and their hands and dropped most of the wheat between the garage and the coop, in a long golden trail from the hen's coop to the garage door.

"The wheat cannot be salvaged from the sand now. Better cover it up with the sand so that we don't get a lot of ants or rats coming for it," said Grandpa.

But their Dad had a better idea. "I will shovel the wheat and sand into a separate bucket and over time we can sprinkle it in the coop. The hens will scratch out the wheat from the sand and nothing will go to waste."

So for the next hour, he shovelled and shovelled all the wheat with the sand, from the coop back to the garage and filled two or three buckets with the mix. It was back breaking work, but he did it slowly and methodically, and collected as much as he could. The shovel too was heavy, but he did not grumble. Their Mum went out to help their Dad and they worked in tandem collecting and cleaning up the mess.

Later, the girls were punished and not given any Fanta with dinner or dessert after dinner. Grandma made them stand on the side steps and look at the quantity of wheat they had wasted. It was only when they stood on the steps that they realised their foolishness and utter waste of so many kilos of wheat.

Their parents had tight lines of anger around their lips and there would have been a lot to answer for by the girls, if their grandparents had not intervened. Who would have believed that these strong and caring parents would be reduced to powerless patients in a couple of decades with the dreaded Parkinson's disease, lying helplessly in bed while they had to be turned and lifted from the bed onto the wheelchair and back.

Picking Fruits

One evening while all were sitting around the table enjoying their tea and *pakoras,* everyone wondered where Samara had disappeared to. "Does anyone know where Samara is?" asked Grandma, while their Mum said, "She probably has gone into the coop to pick up the freshly-laid eggs."

Dad did a quick search of the house and the hen coop, looking through the bedroom windows. No signs of Samara anywhere and everyone was beginning to worry.

"She is probably up in the loft up to something," thought Sabrina and inched towards the steps leading up to the loft to check. She quietly crept up the wooden stairs and once she reached the top, she waited for her eyes to get used to the dark, as she scanned the huge loft.

Sitting astride a beam was Samara, quietly spooning a wood-apple into her mouth, savouring every mouthful. Her grandmother had mashed some jaggery into the wood-apple and she obviously did not want to share it with anyone, least of all Sabrina.

Suddenly Sabrina saw her sister's figure in the distance, towards the end of the roof. "There you are! Why can't you answer? We have all been so worried about you. What are you doing there in the corner, sitting all alone?"

"Shut up! Don't come any closer," shouted Samara as she spooned in another mouthful of the wood-apple. "Leave me alone!"

"No, come down, everyone has been worried about you."

"No, I won't!" said Samara stubbornly, stepping out blindly as she got to her feet. In a flash she had fallen through the false ceiling made of thick fabric painted white and landed on the dining table in a heap. Shocked faces stared at her from around the table as she landed, followed by her bowl and spoon.

"All my wood-apple has been wasted," cried Samara looking at the mess on the floor.

"Up, young lady," said an angry Dad. "Into the corner with you and no tea or wood-apple for the rest of the holiday."

"But first, go and get the broom and sweep up the mess you have made. No one is going to clean up after you!"

Meanwhile their Dad climbed up the loft to pull up the cloth of the false ceiling for the night, which was torn and needed expert repairs. "I will go and look for someone to repair and sort out the tear tomorrow," said their Dad.

"Thankfully the child was not hurt and fell on the table so that broke her fall," said Grandpa.

But Grandma, who had a great sense of humour, started laughing, which made the whole family follow suit. In a matter of minutes the whole house resounded with laughter, thinking of what had happened and were probably relieved that Samara had not been hurt by the escapade.

"Who said girls are less naughty than boys," said their Grandma looking at the girls fondly and taking them into the storeroom for some goodies.

Holidays in Bangalore with the paternal grandparents were fun too, in spite of the fact that they were so much older. This was because their Dad was the youngest sibling in his family. Most often the girls were told to play in the garden rather than make a noise in the house. So, they made friends with the neighbours who were an Army family renting the house. The girls jumped in and made friends and soon they were swapping fruit with each other.

"What are these fruits?" asked Sabrina, looking at a tall tree with thin oval-shaped leaves and beautiful white pom-poms for flowers.

"Look, these are the fruits," said the neighbour, "My Mum calls them rose-apples. They have two large brown seeds in them and not much flesh."

So the girls swapped a bag of avocados for a bag of rose-apples to share with the family.

"Why don't you think of planting the seeds and then we can have our own rose-apple tree," said their Dad.

"That will take at least 10 years to start fruiting," said their grandfather. "So much easier to share with the neighbours and swap our fruit with theirs," he said wisely with a twinkle in his eye.

However, Sabrina did plant a couple of seeds in an old bucket which sprouted and grew into a small tree, which she put down into the soil in her farm many, many decades later and it still grows and fruits, bringing back memories of her childhood.

Avocados too grew on three trees in the garden in Bangalore and the girls were taught how to harvest only the large fruit. For some reason Sabrina could never climb trees, but Samara learned to shimmy up all the trees and was able to help with picking the fruit.

The large storeroom was where the fruit was left to ripen and the girls checked them everyday, to see if they were soft and ready to be eaten. Most of the avocados were large and at least 250gms each fruit.

"Peel the skin off carefully, then cut the fruit in half without hurting the seed in the centre," said Grandma.

"Put the halves on the plate and use a fork to mash up the flesh. Then sprinkle a teaspoon of sugar, or as much as you require on the mash, squeeze a bit of lime and then sit and enjoy it!"

They were very filling fruits and most often the girls shared one fruit, but their mother enjoyed them too and could eat a whole one in a single sitting. That was one fruit Sabrina missed when she got older and the trees were cut down to replace the old colonial home with a block of apartments.

Strong Shoulders

Ten minutes before it was time to leave for the service in church, their Dad walked down to the garage where the car was parked. He was nattily turned out in his tweed jacket which had been tailored for him by the Italian brothers in a nearby community. A good-looking man, her father made sure all of them took care of the way they were turned out, especially for service. Going for Sunday Mass was a ritual the family enjoyed both in Delhi and Shillong. And, even though the Church was within walking distance, the Standard Herald was taken for its weekly spin as Dad was keen on running the car to maintain its battery.

He would take the car out and shine it up himself. And would be waiting for all of the family to come out and pile in. Very often Sabrina noticed that even after putting away the bucket and rag used to clean the car, her Dad would lean across the bonnet of the car and shine it up with a 'kerchief from his pocket.

"Don't do that, Charlie," Mum would admonish, but he would unthinkingly put a dab of spit to shine it perfectly while Mum and the girls would let out a collective moan! The moan was because the same muddy handkerchief was used to wipe their mouths or faces, mop up the sweat on his brow and given generously to their mother to daub her upper lip if the car heated up.

The car roared up the hill to the parking area in front of the church. Then they all filed into the church and sat down in one pew waiting for Mass to begin and listening to the organ music wafting down from the choir loft before the celebrant made his entrance.

The church was built like a replica of the shrine of Lourdes. Lourdes, a French town, has the most famous healing shrine in the world and one of the most popular pilgrimage sites that people of all faiths visited hoping for a miracle cure. When a young village girl named Bernadette Soubirous claimed to see a radiant vision of a woman in white on February 11, 1858, Lourdes was a small market town virtually unknown to the larger world. Over the next five months the lady would appear 17 more times to Bernadette, visions that the Roman Catholic Church (though initially sceptical) would declare authentic appearances of the Virgin Mary. Miraculous cures have been associated with Lourdes ever since, and today the town welcomes more than five million pilgrims a year.

The church had a beautiful grotto built in the style of Lourdes and came to life whenever the church had a celebration of any feast. The feast the girls remembered most vividly was held on November 2, All Souls Day, when an enormous candle-light procession wound its way up the hill to the cemetery.

Their Mum always bought a big packet of candles and helped us girls light them and put them on the candle stands around the grotto. Her hands were perfectly steady without even a quiver as a give-away, of what was in store for her.

"Give me your candles Sabrina or you will pour that hot wax on your palms and cry for hours after that," her Mum would say taking away Sabrina's share of candles.

Sabrina never felt affronted, as she was a bit clumsy lighting the candles and putting them down on the stand. Ever so often the melted candle wax spilled onto her fingers, if slightly tilted and hot wax on your fingers was not a pleasant experience. But she loved seeing the flickering flames, being buffeted around in the breeze in front of the grotto, on the huge candle stands. She felt a sense of calm descend on her as she looked up at the beautiful statue with its gentle and tender expression.

"Let's head home before the rain comes down and we freeze in the November chill," announced their Dad and the girls were glad to jump into the car as even their warm sweaters and thick stockings did nothing against the chill of the hills.

Jumping into the car they enjoyed their Dads habit of switching off the car engine as he took the slope down to the main road. The slope curved around the hill and was pretty steep, keeping the momentum of the moving car, as it zoomed downwards. Then to the girls' utter delight, their Dad would put the car in gear and with a *vroom vroom* the car would spring to life. That would help brake the speed going down and onto the main road. But sadly would slow the car down to a crawl, with the gears holding it back. But by then, the girls had got their thrill for the evening.

The family then had to cross the road in front of the Loreto Convent, which was next door to the church. Then, they got onto the road heading home through the narrow road snaking through the plum orchards and the quaint wooden bridges that covered the the rapidly flowing streams below. The plum trees were covered with delicate pink and some even had white flowers. The blooms did not last for long and soon there were drifts of petals making carpets, under the trees and also on the road along the orchard. Dainty and fragile, the petals wafted onto the road with the breeze, to the delight of the girls. Soon the trees in the orchard would be covered with tiny fruit and even when the trees groaned with fruit, the girls did not try to steal some, because they had their own little orchard of plum trees in their back garden, going down the hillside.

"Go check if the fruits are getting ready," instructed Mum when they came home from school. The girls didn't need to be told twice by Mum, they were out there in a flash, checking the fruit and picking a few ripe, juicy plums to sample. Their very first year in Shillong, they were astonished to find carpets of fruits on the ground, at the base of the tree. Ripe, delicious plums which just lay there and rotted into the ground, as everyone had their own trees with a surfeit of fruit. It was a veritable fruit paradise in Shillong.

Every room had a chest of drawers and since there was so much of fruit they were told to collect the ones on the trees which were firm and semi ripe and put them in the drawers. But the ripe ones from the ground were washed and checked before they were slurped down, juice dripping off their chins and enjoyed, before spitting out the seeds.

"Don't pluck the raw fruit," warned their Dad, "Check if they are completely plum coloured before you pick them."

Sabrina especially loved the large Japanese plums and there were only two trees in the garden with them. The fruits were large and very fleshy and juicy. "Those will make an excellent jam," said their Mum, "So please do not gobble them all up."

"Look Dad, shall I pluck those fruits?" said Sabrina pointing to some high up in the tree.

"Sure! Come, I will lift you up so you can easily get them," said Dad, hoisting her up on his shoulders with one swift and strong movement. No quiver or shiver in his hands holding her as he helped her get at the fruit on the top of the tree.

The dreaded Parkinson's was nowhere on the horizon but much later, when researching the disease, Sabrina realised that it probably was already eating into his nervous system and into her mother's as well. A deadly and silent killer of the human spirit.

To The Factory

Once the fruit started ripening, the large quantities of fruit coming into the house was staggering. Even though all four of them ate their fill, there was still too much ripe fruit in the drawers. So, one morning Mum called Samara to walk down the hill with her.

"Come with me Samara, I want to take a walk down to the canning factory just over the little bridge to check it out. I was told in the convent about the factory which is run by the government and we can go and get our extra fruit canned there for a very minimal amount."

Sabrina let out a wail as she wanted to go along as well. "No, you will stay behind and finish your homework," said Mum. So Sabrina flounced inside to sit at her desk and pretend to complete her homework.

Off went Samara and her mother, to check on the rates and find out how they could use their excess plums, while Samara was curious to see what the whole canning process entailed. They walked into a bright and airy factory which was spick and span but smelled of ripe fruit. Everywhere were baskets of plums and pineapples and curiously they saw large plastic packets of sugar.

"This is a government run factory and so our costs

are very minimal," explained Scott Sangma the smiling manager in-charge.

"I have around 20 kilos of ripe, very good quality plums at home and I want to make jam of them," said Mum to the manager.

"That would take about half an hour to make and once it's made we need to let it cool. Then we can it and charge you for the making and the canning. You have to bring us your sugar," said the manager.

"How much sugar do I need for 20 kilos of fruit?" asked Sabrina's mother.

"Depends on the sweetness of the fruit. If they are sweet and juicy we require one kg of sugar for 2 kilos of fruit. Otherwise one kilo for every kilo of fruit."

"That sounds good! When can I bring my fruit and the sugar to you?" asked their Mum.

"We have too much to finish today, but if you come in by 10am tomorrow with all your fruit and sugar we will get started on your jam production first, for the day."

"What about the bottles, will you supply those as well?"

"We are a canning factory, so we will seal your jam in tins and we charge for the cans, but they are easy to transport. You have to tell us if you want the jam in one or two kilo tins."

Mum could not stop smiling as she walked home holding Samara's hand and saying, "What fun, I must call Dad in the office and tell him our news. He can organise the sugar for me so that we can take the fruit and sugar down first thing in the morning."

"Let's walk quickly and tell Sabrina, I am sure she will be

excited to hear our news."

In the distance they could see the name board of the house swinging in the breeze in the front verandah. The house was curiously called 'Charing Cross' but all of them did not know the connection of the name with London, as no one had travelled there yet. The name was carved and painted into a very creatively painted piece of wood, which had scallops along the edges and was hung up with chains attached and screwed into the wooden beam, above the steps to the entrance.

Samara raced inside to tell Sabrina who was most excited and insisted that Mum take her when she was going the next day.

"I need to come and see what they will do. I have never been to a jam making factory," said Sabrina.

"Let's check all the trees one last time and collect all the fruit, so we don't waste any, once we take the fruit to the factory," replied Mum.

So the girls went down to the fruit garden, which ran down the length of the hill on the side of the house and collected all the fruit that had not been picked off the trees.

The next morning Dad helped take the fruit in the car along with the one kilo packets of sugar he had bought and they all piled in and rolled down the hill to the factory.

Scott Sangma greeted them, a smile all over his plump face and the girls excitedly helped to weigh the fruit. After which women in white caps took the fruit and washed them clean and once they were weighed, they were put into large stainless steel vats. The sugar was mixed into the fruit and the electric vats began to hum. A flat stirrer also worked by electricity, spun round and round mixing the jam.

"Stay away from the machines," said Mr. Sangma when the girls edged towards them. "Unless you want to be boiled and made into jam too," he said with a laugh.

"What are those tins?" their Dad asked Mr. Sangma.

"Those are two kilo tins of pineapple slices," said Sangma, "we tinned those yesterday."

"I would love to make a few tins of those as well," said their Mum excitedly.

"You will have to drive down to the government nursery and there they are selling them for a rupee a fruit. Bring us around 20 fruits and I will make you two or three large tins of pineapple slices. You will also have to bring me sugar."

"Let's drive down and buy the pineapples and sugar," said their Dad and they all piled into the Standard Herald and were off with a roar.

"Look for nice bright yellow and ripe fruit," instructed Sangma and so that's exactly what they did. "Pick up and smell only the ripe fruit and the yellower they are, the better for canning."

"Here are our fruit and the sugar Mr. Sangma," said their Dad on their return to the factory and the two men smiled while the fruit exchanged hands.

"The pineapples are cored and the skin is removed, so one is not left with much fruit," explained Mr Sangma. "Leave everything with me and come back tomorrow, everything has to be properly cooled before we tin them."

"Let's go home now and have lunch," said their Dad as the girls piled into the car. "I have got some ice-cream for girls who behave and Rosy has made chicken momos and noodles for lunch," to the girls excited squeals of delight, as the car wended it's way home.

"Press the horn Dad," said the girls and he did, making the horn sound like a trumpet, which heralded their arrival home.

Sabrina remembered clearly how well her Dad would firmly pull up the lever of the brake, which would make a crunching sound as it engaged and kept the car steady on the steep incline in front of the house. And her Mum would effortlessly carry Samara up the steps of the house if ever she was tired and cranky and refused to walk.

The Old Homestead

Holidays were always a big deal with Sabrina and Samara's parents. They always escaped from the heat of New Delhi for a month when they were posted there. And the girls loved their holidays especially in Goa, in the village where their ancestors came from, in Pilerne, Bardez, Goa. Whenever they went to live in the old homestead, the plan was to stay in the house for a month at least. It was not easy for their mother who was an out and out city bred girl from Mumbai, so she did not enjoy the old homestead, with it's creepy crawlies and insects. This was because the house was kept locked for most of the year and her father came down to just keep an eye on it.

"Move back, let me open the front door," said their Dad. And the huge old door creaked open on its hinges. The ancient old teak doors did not have modern hinges but were fixed on large spikes that rolled around when opened. A tiny little orange frog jumped off the name plate which their Dad had fixed on the front door.

"Eeeee!" yelled Samara in fright and jumped away, hiding behind Sabrina while they both looked at the little orange creature, as it jumped enormous leaps across the verandah and out into the wilderness beyond the house.

"That frog is endemic to the Western Ghats and you are so lucky to see a real live one," said her Dad most matter-of-factly as he pulled the door open. "Now tonight you will hear a big chorus of them singing out in the fields. You need to just enjoy the sound and not be afraid. They are afraid of us big, enormous human beings."

"Come on, help carry the bags into the house," instructed their Mum. "Put them onto that chair and then we can decide which room we are going to be in."

"Let's open the windows up too," said their Dad. "And let the fresh air into the house. The poor house has been locked up for so many months."

"Uh, I can't carry this bag," said Sabrina grumbling. "It's way too heavy for me."

"Leave the bags alone and go and help your mother with the windows," said Dad, easily lifting all the bags into the house.

"There are brooms in the dining room, so let's quickly clean up the house and then walk down to Jack's for lunch. I wrote and informed him in advance that we needs meals from today," said Dad.

"Oh no! My broom looks like it is half eaten by white ants," cried Samara.

"Yes, that's the problem with Goa. White ants eat up everything, and destroy all the beams in the roof and that is why so many houses in Goa have fallen down," explained their Mum, as she tried to collect a whole heap of cobwebs and dirt into her dust-pan.

"Eeeeeeeeeee!" Went Samara yet again, racing to hide behind her Dad this time. "What is it Samara? Will you stop squealing and frightening the poor old house?"

"Look! Look! There's a crazy little insect which is racing around the bedroom on hundreds of little legs," shouted Samara.

"That's a millipede, and it really is quite harmless Samara," said their Dad. "Look, I will work some magic with it!" And he just touched the little crawling insect that immediately spun itself into a tight concentric circle of body and legs. Then her father just nonchalantly picked it up and threw it out to freedom, out the window.

As the little family cleaned up the musty smelling house, their Dad pointed to the pictures of their Grandfather with his distinguished moustache and delicate featured Grandmother along with a beetling eye-browed Great Grandfather on the walls in the high-roofed hall.

"Who is that girl, Dad?" asked Sabrina, pointing to a picture of a girl standing, dressed formally in stockings and closed shoes near a table. "That was my sister who died of typhoid when she was barely twelve. In those days there was no penicillin as yet and so we lost her right here in Goa."

Both girls often looked up at the picture when they walked in the hall during the holiday feeling sorry for the girl who was around their age, whose life was cut-short and she never enjoyed growing up and becoming an adult.

The toilet was the only part of the holiday that the girls disliked as they had to go into a building which was outside the house. Inside the building large piles of firewood were stacked for the use of the house-hold. But the "toilet" was just a raised platform with a large hole in it. The girls normally liked going together, as the hut was dingy and dark and strange rustling sounds came from the piles of wood.

Sitting down one morning side by side, they heard the grunts of the pigs who scavenged the faeces and that is how the toilets were kept clean. "I hate those things," said Samara one day. "They make me scared in case they reach up and bite me."

"I'll be back," she said to Sabrina and ran out of the hut for a few minutes coming back brandishing a lit broom stick, which she had pulled out of the coconut broom. She had lit the end by sticking it into the flames of the wood stove in the kitchen. In minutes the pig was back snuffling around in the bottom of the toilet, when Samara stuck the lit broom-stick into the poor thing's nose.

It ran out squealing in pain and Dad came running to check, thinking the girls had fallen in or got hurt. When he realised what Samara had done both girls were sent to stand inside the storeroom, in the house in silence. Punished for one hour.

"Don't you know if you burn the pig, it won't come back and the toilets will be left filthy and smelling?" said their Dad.

"How could you be so silly?" asked Mum, equally angry.

But both girls instead of being chastised, stood in the room convulsed with laughter, tears of mirth pouring down their faces, much to their parents' annoyance. It was only after a few days that the whole family had a good laugh about Samara's escapade, but she was sternly warned never to try it again.

For years, it was a story told around the family table by the girls and their parents. And much later too when the girls had their own children, the story had become part of family lore.

The Promise

"I have to carry my spikes to practice my starts in the stadium on them," shouted Sabrina as she left the house carrying her new spikes slung over her shoulder, taking the short cut to the National Stadium near the India Gate. "Coach Balbir Singh wants me to work on my sprint starts for the upcoming Athletic Meet."

"He says if I nail the start, I will have the race in my pocket. A good start will give me the advantage of a few seconds over my competitors and push me out in the front of the pack."

"Yes, he is right. Go practice your start over and over again till you perfect it. That's the only way you can win," said her Dad who had been the Mysore State Champion while he was in Engineering College in Bangalore.

Every evening Sabrina would pick up her spikes and walk down to the stadium with Samara for regular athletics practice. Once in a while, her Dad would turn up on his scooter straight from work on odd occasions, still in his Air Force uniform, to watch them practising.

"This meet if you come first and break a record, I will buy you a pair of starting blocks," promised her Dad.

So that gave Sabrina the added impetus to work on her starts and she was up for the challenge of coming first and trying to break the record. The day of the State Meet dawned and both Sabrina's parents came to watch her participate in the under 15 Junior girls 100 and 200 metres race.

"Calling all participants in the Under 15 Junior Girls 100 metre race," crackled the announcers voice, over the sketchy sound system.

"Come on Dad, I have to go, it's my race being announced," said Sabrina jumping up and beginning to slip down her skirt, to compete in her school shorts and school blouse.

"Yes go Sabrina, but don't rush across the field as the Javelin event is on and be careful as you cross the area, to get to your start," warned her Mum.

Sabrina's Dad picked up her spikes and walked towards the field with Sabrina in tow. "It's better to put them on on the grass rather than here as you could dislodge a spike while walking on cement."

Her Dad walked purposefully towards the starting line and then gave her the spikes when they reached the 100 metre start position. "Sit down comfortably and put them on," he instructed Sabrina, who sat on the grass and pulled on the spikes. "Tie the long laces firmly, to avoid them opening and tripping you during the race," said Dad.

Having her father come along with her for her first State Meet gave Sabrina a lot of courage as her father exuded confidence and strength. In fact when she got ready for the start of the race, her father's advice rang in her ears. "Focus and take off as soon as the gun goes off, because if you get the start, you win the race."

He had been a Mysore State athlete and whatever advice he was giving her, was from personal experience.

Sabrina knew if she followed his instructions she would definitely emerge a winner. In fact, he would take her on the front lawn of the Officers Mess where they lived and make her practice her starts under his personal guidance, every single day. Giving the girls a head start in life was the only focus of both mother and father, since they had already achieved so much themselves.

That State Meet, Sabrina not only broke the Junior Girls 100 metres, 200 metres and Long Jump records, to her utter amazement she also won the overall Champions trophy. Her parents were thrilled for her and there was a feeling of elation and triumph in her heart when Sabrina achieved what she had set out to.

"Okay, since you were promised a pair of starting blocks if you achieved your goal, come on lets go to Rakhra, the best sports shop in Connaught Place, and buy them," said Dad.

So while Samara and Mum headed home, Sabrina was taken to the sports store to buy her the promised starting blocks.

"You did not have to fight too much to reach the first place," said her Dad as they whizzed towards Connaught Place on his scooter.

"No Dad, I got a good start that had me out before the other competitors, and I did focus to finish the race, as quickly as I could," said Sabrina.

The shop smelled of leather and linseed oil used on cricket bats. It was like a huge storehouse of wonderful sports goods and it was Sabrina's first visit, so she stared at everything on display.

"Could I see your range of starting blocks?" asked her

Dad of the smiling attendant who came forward to serve them.

"Yes, sure Sir! This way please," and he led them to a stand behind the cricket bats and near the hockey sticks.

"I would like some starting blocks for my daughter to use for her sprints," asked her Dad.

"She is tall enough to use an adult size," he said and pulled out a set of blocks with a light aluminium frame. There was a strip of ridged rubber, stuck down on the rectangular blocks themselves, into which her spikes got lodged for the start.

"You have to adjust the distance between the feet and then tighten the screws down to hold them firmly in place," advised the salesman.

"I would like my daughter to try them first before we think of buying them," stated her Dad.

"Sure, Sir! Let her try them her on this coir strip of mat," agreed the salesman with a smile.

Sabrina had never used blocks before, but in a matter of minutes she knew what she had to do and they were able to move the pieces and screw them down, according to her height.

Using the blocks for the first time in the National Games which Sabrina was selected for, helped her get the bronze medal and make her the third fastest girl under 15 in India. It had been exciting for her to be feted by her coach and the other athletes from her state.

Promises were meant to be kept and decades later when Sabrina told her son, "Get a seat in the US for your medical residency, and I will give you my savings of

10 lakhs to go." He got the seat and she kept her word.

That was the solid support provided by their parents, in all they did right through their growing years. No matter what she wanted to try her hand at they were always there to buttress and sustain. So when her Dad first began to show signs of unsteadiness later in life, it was terrifying for the girls to witness and internalise that it was a condition that could never be reversed. There was no cure found as yet.

Two Graves

While Sabrina and Samara were still in school one day, Sabrina was collected and brought home by her father. "What's the matter Dad?" asked Sabrina. "Why are you bringing me home when it's not even lunch time?"

Her father was silent and said nothing to her. He just held her hand tightly and walked with his head down quite unlike his usual chatty self. Sabrina wondered what was going on but she could sense this was a time to avoid any questions and rein in her typical irrelevant questioning. A sense of maturity seemed to creep into her with every step and when she saw the big crowd as Dad opened the gate her puzzlement grew.

"So sorry to hear the news," said an old friend, coming forward to hug Dad.

"She is in a better place and free from pain at last," said the priest from the local church who had visited the family for decades.

"It is hard, but with time the pain will subside," consoled another friend. And she was shocked and surprised to see Dad crying. She knew that he was extremely fond of his quiet and gentle mother. His big messy handkerchief came out and he wiped his face and blew his nose.

People started speaking to Dad, but as she ascended the steps of the house which strangely had the front doors wide open, her eyes perceived her grandmother laid out in the hall, and her stillness and her mother's red rimmed eyes confirmed her biggest fears. Grandmother was dead.

The enormity and finality of death hit her young mind only then and she stood to one side of the bier, quietly holding the hand of one of her uncles, while her parents organised the entire funeral. It was a very traumatic time and Sabrina realised that and waited patiently till her sister returned. Two years younger Samara was unable to understand the enormity of what had occurred. She could see that her grandmother was rather still and unmoving. People were sobbing and crying around her and the domestic help in the house sat around on the floor, wailing periodically.

All around the bier were pots of spider lilies from the garden and a smell of eau de cologne permeated the air. After that day, Sabrina hated spider lilies, as they reminded her of the death and the loss of her grandmother.

"Close the doors," said their Dad, to the domestic help, of the intervening doors leading to his father's room. "Don't let him know what has happened, we can break it to him slowly after the funeral and burial is over."

Both the grandparents had been very frail and weak for a long time and had not interacted at all, but obviously had been aware of each other's presence in neighbouring rooms.

"What has happened to Mum?" her grandfather questioned their Dad when he returned from the funeral and burial. "I can smell eau de cologne on you," he said to

Dad. "You never use that; why, why, what has happened? Why are you dressed in black?"

But their Dad was unable to tell him sensing that he might lose his other parent too.

Little did the girls expect their grandfather to pass away seven days later, when he guessed the news, from the sounds beyond his door. His Parkinson's had been very pronounced with helplessly shaking hands and he had needed help for everything. A boy had been employed to assist him with all his needs, and from a cauldron of fragmented memories Sabrina remembered his slow, shuffling, forward-stooping walk to and from the toilet.

Dad organised everything for both funerals and held himself erect through the entire proceedings of both highly charged and emotional burials. Never once did he break down and he even had the energy to provide a meal, to all the mourners who had come from far and wide as is the custom after the burial. Sabrina's memories were cemented only later when she was taken along with Samara to the cemetery to view the grave which her father had arranged for both of them. A large grave, covering two sites, where they were interred side by side. An amazing paean by a son devoted to his parents and who never failed to show it.

But she also had happier memories of her father's parents over the years, when they came from New Delhi and Shillong, for their family vacations to Bangalore. The garden was large and gave them ample leg room to run around and here too there was a large chicken coop with Leghorn hens. The birds were white in colour and laid a continuous stream of eggs in a room, to the side of their run.

One morning when the girls were out playing in the garden while the adults sat around the dining table sipping tea and chatting, Samara in her curiosity opened the door to the coop and sneaked in to collect eggs as she did in Baroda, not realising the eggs were easily accessible through the room at the side. In minutes the entire garden was filled with white hens with red combs, running around the garden, happily eating up plant leaves and excited to be free to run around.

Hearing the commotion their Mum, Dad and all the helpers rushed out and everyone ran around to herd the hens back into the coop. They had rushed about everywhere in the garden and some had even landed in the rose bushes in the front. The dogs joined in the fun making mock charges at the hens who fled, wings outstretched, racing hither and thither.

"Now which of you girls let the hens out?" shouted their Dad, grabbing one of the hens that was busily scratching out a bulb in the lilly patch.

No one replied, but it took more than half an hour to round up all the birds and close the door, behind the last squawking fowl.

"You girls are so badly behaved and have caused too much trouble," said their Mum in a stern voice. "Get inside the house and into your rooms, and sit there reading till you are called for lunch."

Both parents were into their early forties and there was no signs of any shake or tremor in either of their hands. Their grandfather too was in his sixties but he sat at the head of the table and presided over it. There was no signs of any frailty and spoke with a clear and kind voice.

One holiday they were all sitting around the dining

table enjoying the ripe mangoes off the Malgova tree in the garden. Everyone could go into the storeroom, off the dining room where hundreds of mangoes had been spread, across the floor to ripen in some hay. The wonderful smell of ripe mangoes filled the room and the girls were excited to be able to go in and choose their own fruit. Then they took it to their grandfather, who cut them into slices and then gave them to the girls to devour.

"Bring those cheeks of the mangoes to me," said Samara's grandmother to her, who rushed to her with the fruit .

"See this is the easiest way to eat them," she said, slicing the flesh inside the skins into neat squares. "Now take a spoon and spoon the squares into your mouths."

Even if they wanted to eat a second mango considering they were so large, their grandfather never stopped them. "They are all for us to enjoy. Go and help yourself," he would say to the girls' inordinate excitement.

"Stop being greedy, one is quite enough," said their Dad. But their grandfather always stepped in and let them have as many as they wanted, like a true benign grandfather.

Blooming Flowers

Everything for the wedding of the girls was home-made. The family just got together on the dining table in the house in Bangalore, where her parents had retired, and worked as a team to creatively make all the church and hall decorations.

"I want wood-roses for my wedding decorations," said Samara. "Wood-roses that we can grow in the garden and once they are dry I will paint silver."

"That's a lot of wood-roses," said their Dad. "We have a year to organise growing them."

There was a wood-rose vine already in the garden, growing along a fence. Their Dad decided to grow another on the back wall so that they got enough blooms to use in both the large St. Patrick's Church and the sprawling Air-force Officers mess.

The Wood-Rose *Argyreia nervosa* is a native of India. Interestingly, the plant is a cousin of the Morning glory, and its flowers resemble the morning glory flowers except that they are yellow. Wood-roses aren't 'roses' at all, in fact they aren't any kind of flower, but rather they're a vine's thin-walled, capsular fruits, with much enlarged, dried-out, stiff, irregularly-incised sepals. Inside each egg-size capsule, four black, fuzzy seeds are suspended and rattle around when moved.

So once the flowers bloom and the 'wood-roses' form and dry on the vine, they can be snipped off and used on a lot of flower arrangements.

"I will cut the wood-roses off myself," said Samara who had the gift of arranging flowers from her childhood. "I want to plan how much of the vine I want as well, to add to the arrangement," she said.

Once the wood-roses formed and they were ready to be taken off, Samara clipped them attached to the vine, so they could be affixed, to the back of her arrangements easily, with some flexible wire. The roses were hand painted silver by her Dad and left to dry in the storeroom of the house. Later on the day of the wedding, her arrangements were made with fresh red roses added alongside the silver wood-roses and made a stunning display, in both the church and the hall.

Creativity had been encouraged by their parents and home-made was preferred, rather than just going out to the shops and buying ready-made things.

Samara was also a very creative cook and handled most of the cooking once the girls grew up, as their mother was not very adroit in the kitchen. Anything she cooked was delectable and quite flavourfully inventive. She had an ingenious and imaginative style of cooking even a simple *daal* which the entire family thoroughly enjoyed.

At Christmas time, her *marzipan* sweets and date-roll came out far better than her Mum's. And her fruit cake too for Christmas was inspired and original. The whole family gathered round when it was time to make *chaklis,* the smell literally permeated the house.

"If you eat them all up, there will be none left for the tin," she scolded when her Dad swiped a third—or was it a fourth—*chakli* from the cooling pile.

A hard slap on the wrists when it was Sabrina who slunk in to steal her stash.

"Mum, at this rate we'll have none left for Christmas!" She yelled out for support and Mum shooed the pair away and closed the kitchen door.

All the Christmas sweets were made and had to be locked away by her mother in a trunk made of tin, till the 24th night. Then when the family returned from Midnight Mass, along with glasses of wine they sat down to plundering the trunk of all the goodies.

Sabrina was never a great cook and she never tried hard to learn either, as Samara outshone her when it came to making any dish. Plus several king-sized disasters, put her off even trying to cook.

"Is that called a chocolate cake?" their Dad asked with a huge grin, when Sabrina tried her hand at making an easy sounding chocolate cake.

The cake for some reason never rose and instead just sank into a volcanic hole, when she kept it out to cool. That was as far as Sabrina's trials at cooking were.

What was great support was their Dad, jumping onto the scooter, to go and purchase all the ingredients, which he very willingly did. Their Mum too was ready to lend a hand and the whole family ganged up together, to enjoy eating and cooking through the holiday season.

The Funeral

Sabrina and Samara both married in their early twenties and had babies of their own when they were fairly young. Sabrina lived in the crosshairs of chaos especially when her boys were inoculated or down with a bug.

"Just put them into the car and come here," her Mum would instruct. "They will be happy in the garden."

With so many hands to help, Sabrina would calm down in a matter of minutes of coming to see her parents and for some reason, the boys too were happier spending time visiting with their grandparents.

This was photograph time for her Dad, who immediately went in to bring out his camera and take pictures. "Gino, look at Grandpa and smile," her father would say, taking spontaneous shots of the boys in action, playing out in the garden.

One day Dad returned home from Russell Market with an enormous crab for lunch. The mandibles or pincers of the large greenish river crab were 'fixed' by piercing a stick through the side of each claw. As he parked his scooter in the verandah at the back of the house, he called out to the little boys, "Come and see what Grandpa has brought for you from the market." That brought the boys thundering up to his scooter, as he pulled it onto the stand.

"See his pincers don't work, and he can't bite you," said her Dad coaxing the scared kids closer. The crab was a feisty fellow and as soon as her Dad put it on the floor, it began to rapidly run sideways towards the door to escape.

"See crabs move sideways, doesn't that look funny?" chuckled Grandma trying to lighten the mood in the room. But the boys were still not convinced, eying the crustacean warily from afar.

"Come help me catch him and bring him back," and they both ran after the scuttling crab. There was an irreverence in her father's tone which slowly reduced the boys fears and soon they were screaming and laughing with him, trying to catch it on the kitchen floor.

"Stop it, stop it," their grandmother shouted. "It will get thin and will have no meat left in it to eat if you chase it around so much."

"Tie it up Grandpa, take this belt and tie it up," and in minutes their grandpa had tied the belt around the crab and the boys held the end and began to take it for 'walks' around the house.

"That's not a pet dog Gino!" scolded their grandma. "Bring it to me to cook for lunch."

"Just one more round," said Gino pulling the crab behind him while Grandpa, doubled up with laughter, took pictures.

"I want to also take it for a walk," said a snivelling Carlos, the smaller boy and off went the crab obligingly, with the second toddler running after it while holding onto the belt.

"That's quite enough," said the boys' Grandma. "It's enough of fun for one day, give it to me. Sabrina take them into the garden for a while so that I can get the lunch organised."

"Maybe we can check if the jackfruit or custard apples are ripe enough to be picked," suggested Grandpa and the two boys obligingly latched on firmly to his warm hands and went down the front steps into the garden.

Coming to her parents large home helped Sabrina transcend all irritation and shortness of patience that she felt with the boys at home. Her parents were always there for her no matter what and that boosted her confidence through the boys growing years.

However, rich food was the norm in her parent's home and snacking on puffs and *samosas* a daily affair. In fact her father loved sandwiches if there were no other snacks to be had.

"Bring me the butter," he would ask Carlos or Gino, "from the fridge."

Willing little chubby legs would run towards the fridge and take out the bread and the 500gms block of Amul butter to give him.

Then taking a sharp knife their grandfather would slice a thick wedge of the golden-yellow butter and put it between two really fresh slices of bread, and that was considered a sandwich. Their grandfather would divide one sandwich into two for the boys and sit back and enjoy several himself.

"Come, climb onto the chair," he would guide the boys, or lift them onto the heavy dining room chairs. Then they would all companionably sit together and eat their sandwiches.

He would pour himself a hot cup of tea that was always ready in the flask kept standing on the dumb waiter, which anyone could help themselves to. Milk and sugar was on the table, covered up with a doily to keep away the flies.

The boys never forgot the years they spent with their grandparents. In fact the bond was so strong that it was only at her father's funeral, very much later, that the depth of their loss came to the surface, just as they were about to inter him. Gino was standing to one side of the pit, into which the casket was to be lowered, with his friends and the family stood on the other side.

Probably the enormity of the finality of death only hit him then, as the casket began to be lowered and to everyone's complete horror he stumbled forward crying, "Grandpa, Grandpa, don't go." This huge six footer completely overcome with grief, hands outstretched towards the man he completely adored. Thankfully his friends were able to restrain him and pull him backwards, to prevent any untoward accident from occurring. That was one image that was burned in Sabrina's mind forever.

"Come sit down Gino," said his friend Michael, "Just hold on to your memories and be grateful for all the fun you had over the years with your Grandpa."

A cauldron of fragmented memories swirled about Gino's head, as he sat on a mound of mud watching them lower the casket into the deep pit in the ground. The worst was yet to come, the thuds of the large clods of soil, which landed all over the beautiful new casket, thrown first by the mourners and then the grave diggers.

Tears poured unchecked down his face, his grief visible even in the angle of his head. He sat their forlorn and submissive to the finality of death.

Gino had watched a strong and able-bodied man reduced to a mere shadow of himself. And towards the end in the hospital and when his grandfather was brought home, he realised the struggle he was going through and the pain and suffering which had turned a strong and able-bodied man into a wreck.

Reading up on the disease when he returned home to his laptop, on the michaeljfox website, he understood that studies show, that some cases of Parkinson's disease are caused by genetic mutations. Hereditary causes of this disease are rare. Only 15 percent of those who have Parkinson's disease have a family history of it. Research suggests that a combination of genetic and environmental factors may cause Parkinson's disease.

In The Garden

The dining table was covered with ISC (Indian School Certificate) answer scripts and the boys Gino and Carlos were helping Grandma "correct" the maps in the Geography papers. They spent long hours helping her and then besides getting heaps of snacks and stuffing their faces, they got some pocket-money which was the icing on the cake.

"I am walking down the road to Sooraj, to get some dosas for all of us," announced Grandpa. "Get me the tiffin carrier and I can bring the *chutney* and the *sambhar* safely in it."

Sabrina's father always walked up the road to buy the *dosas* (rice pancakes) and bring them home, wrapped in newspaper. He carried a cloth bag in which a dozen *dosas*, all wrapped in banana leaves and newspaper were placed in the bag and the *sambhar* (spicy South Indian lentil and vegetable dish) and *chutney* (spicy Indian condiment) filled the tiffin carrier containers.

The table was cleared as soon as the family heard the gate latch being opened and plates were swiftly put out for everyone to sit down and gorge themselves. Then the *dosas* were placed in the centre of the table with the *chutney* and *sambhar* in bowls. Spoons clattered and there was a lot of noise and fun, till everyone sat down. Then, silence reigned as the *dosas* were wolfed down, along with slurps of the *sambhar* and *chutney.*

The inside of every *dosa* was plastered with a red chilly *chutney*, which Sabrina and her Mum, could not stomach. So they used a butter knife to scrape off some and then put back the potato *palya* (spicy potato filling) which was stuffed with savoury slices of onion and a cashew nut or tiny wedges of coconut sometimes.

Everyone took a spoon of the coconut *chutney* and of course a whole lot of the sweetish *sambhar*, into which bits of the *dosa*, were dipped, eaten with their fingers.

"Stop slurping the *sambhar*," Sabrina remonstrated the boys. "And don't eat too much *chutney* or you will have backdoor trots tonight!"

The boys laughed and helped themselves to more, watching Grandpa enjoying his to the last spoonful which the boys imitated, much to Sabrina's disgust.

Hayes Road was a haven for the boys, with grandparents who loved to spoil them and were young enough to take them on holidays with them.

"I have a plan to go to Pilerne next week," announced Grandpa. "Who wants to come with me?" and the boys whooped with excitement.

"Please Mum may we go too?" they begged of Sabrina, who did not mind as she knew they would enjoy any trip to their family home in Pilerne, Goa.

"You boys can come if you finish all your homework, and help me with some stuff in the garden," said Grandpa to twin vigorous head nods.

That was what Sabrina loved about her parents. They were 'soft' on the boys but also firm and got things done rather than give in to everything they demanded.

Helping in the garden meant re-potting the pots, in the front of the house, with compost from the large garden pit. "Come on, bring the *bandlees* and the *mumtee* and let's get down to work," Grandpa said. And the boys went scuttling off to the "storeroom" where all the gardening tools were neatly stacked.

"Let me put on my gum boots," said Grandpa while the boys readied the *bandlees* (buckets) to carry the compost to the front of the garden and brought over the *mumtees* (trowels). "The gum boots are to prevent my feet getting hurt with any sharp glass pieces or tin which may have been inadvertently thrown into the pit by the servants," explained Grandpa.

Jumping in Grandpa dug into the black and earthy smelling compost and yelled out to Gino to bring his garden gloves from the storeroom.

"Always use your gloves when working in the garden," he explained to the boys. "One never knows what weed or insect maybe in the soil which could unnecessarily bother you."

"Oh, I love working with my hands and letting the soil run through my fingers, Grandpa," pooh poohed Carlos, but Gino swiftly curbed him saying, "So you have forgotten how your palm was sliced open in school playing in the sand-pit there?"

Immediately, Carlos recalled the incident when his palm ached for weeks till it healed after being cut open by a dirty piece of glass.

"Pour a mug of water into each pot," said Grandpa. "And leave them to loosen." And off went the boys to carry a big bucket of water, each with empty jam tins, to use as mugs to pour the water.

"Now take that old knife and slide it around the edge of the pot and the whole plant will come out like a cake," said Grandpa.

Carlos tried for the first time, with one pot. The whole pot of ferns that he was trying to re-pot, came up pot and all above the ground. "*Uff!* How annoying is this?" he grumbled while a loud guffaw from Grandpa suggested he run the knife around the edge again and then, put his foot on the edge of the pot and then try his luck.

Carlos fell back laughing holding up the entire fern, with the soil clinging around it with a cap of fine matted roots. "Now you know why we need to re-pot," said Grandpa. "The plant need some fresh soil to grow in and look healthy. And the best medium is this compost which comes out of our kitchens for free."

"Look, look at that big wriggly earthworm," shouted Carlos, as Grandpa dumped a *mumtee* load onto the *bandlee*.

"They are friends of the gardener and totally harmless. Stop acting like funks," admonished Grandpa. "In fact put one or two into the soil as you re-pot the plant, it will keep the soil aerated and healthy," explained Grandpa.

"See! I am holding one," said Gino his hand in the air with his gloved fingers holding up the wriggly pink and brown earthworm.

"Take that knife," said Grandpa, "and cut off most of those roots leaving at least a quarter attached to the plant.

Then put a stone against the hole in the pot, to prevent all the water running out and fill the pot with compost."

The sun was hot and everyone was sweating with the exertion of the exercise, but Grandma's cheerful voice, promising them tall glasses of Mango Fool with ice, encouraged them to get on with the job.

One after the other the pots were cleaned up and re-potted, with some plants being divided into two since they had multiplied over the year. The fresh smelling compost was a new experience for the boys, as they were surprised by the fact that it was just the wet waste from the kitchen which had turned into manure for the plants.

Egg shells, coffee grounds, water melon rind, orange and lime skins, tea leaves and onion skins, all the waste from the kitchen was turned into compost by dumping in the pit with the occasional 'turn' over the week by Grandpa, jumping into the pit with his gum boots. He wielded the *mumtee* expertly digging out the decomposed wet waste which had turned into an earthy smelling compost, lower down in the pit.

The Train Journey

Gino was twelve when his Grandma decided to take him with her to Baroda where her parents lived. The idea of going for the first time by train, filled every waking moment of Gino's mind with excitement. Grandma was going for a fortnight so packing was completed well-ahead of time, with Gino unable to contain his excitement. At the time the dreaded Parkinson's and Alzheimer's had not hit Sabrina's Mum and she was in her prime, teaching in one of the biggest schools in the city. She never taught the young kids, but instead taught the older 11th and 12th standard students. In fact, she went on to do her Master's in Literature when she was in her 50s. How many women will take on a Master's degree at that age, especially here in India, where once you touch 50, women are supposed to fade gently into the background?

Their bags were packed and the day dawned when Gino and his Grandmother were off. This was a long two day journey at the time, and so a lot of food too was packed for the way. First, a train would take them to Guntakal where they would have to change trains to take them to Baroda, as it was called in the day, now changed to Vadodara. Today one can get the Rajkot and a dozen other express trains that take you directly from Yeshwanthpur or Krishnarajapuram to Vadodara in a day.

The train journey was packed with huge crowds of holiday makers, travelling from one part of India to the other. Gino never bothered to learn any language properly, so was at a loose end while travelling. However Sabrina's Mum was comfortable chatting with her fellow travellers in a fluent Hindi. She never learned to speak Tamil with the help in the house, but her Hindi made travelling very easy, as communication was simple for her.

"You need to learn to make friends with all types of people Gino. You can't mix only with your friends all the time. Try and put that Kannada you learned in class to use now," coaxed his Grandma.

Frowning in concentration Gino's mind went back to his Kannada classes and tried his best, to chat with the two young boys, who were sitting with their Mum on the next berth.

"Which school do you go to?" he asked breaking into a smile and trying to strike up a conversation, with the young boys who seemed to speak only Kannada.

It took a bit of understanding, when the boy replied in fluent Kannada, but Gino did try and make a decent conversation, hoping to impress the boy's mother who had a large mound of *methi chappaties*, stashed in her food basket.

Gino's grandmother warned him, about was not going near the open doors of the compartment, as he could fall out with the strong rocking of the train. And she instructed him to call her when he went to the toilet, as the hole in the toilet which served as a commode was also dangerous and he could lose a shoe or slipper through the wide hole.

Most often the toilet was stinking and so Gino did not use it much and he wondered why his grandmother, probably used it just twice through the entire two days. There was plenty of water which was topped up at the larger stations, but people were inherently dirty and all the toilets were stinking and foul to use, as people did not care to clean up after themselves.

The woman on the berth in front finally shared her *methi chappaties* with them, while Sabrina's Mum offered them their *chutney* sandwiches. "Grandma, please don't give them any more," said Gino with a frown, seeing the five kids of the family pounce on his Grandmother's sandwiches.

"Take another *chappatie* Gino," admonished his Grandma. "We must learn to share. It is also important that we learn new flavours and tastes. Take a piece of the mango pickle and eat it with the *chappatie*, its delicious."

Gino's grandparents had travelled all over India on Grandpa's postings and so they enjoyed a varied palate and did not just hang on to their own Goan cuisine. In fact Grandma cooked North Indian food as well as her Goan speciality, Sorpotel.

When the train reached Sholapur Gino's grandmother wanted a cup of tea and a few slices of *dhokla*, a Gujarati delicacy which reminded her of home. She gave him a ten rupee note and sent him to the stall, just outside their compartment on the station. Gino was excited to be able to stretch his legs and get off the train. In a few minutes he got the highly sweetened tea, in an earthen pot and two large slices of *dhokla*, draped with slit green chilly and rushed back to Grandma who was waiting anxiously at the open door.

"I have to go back and get my tea," he yelled, pushing the *dhokla* into her waiting hands and quickly rushing back to the stall to collect his tiny mud pot of tea.

"Good for you, Gino!" said Grandma. "You managed to get us everything with still some time to spare."

They went back to sit and enjoy their tea in the compartment and only after a while did the train driver, blow his warning whistle and then they were off again. All over the floor Gino noticed that the kids from the other berth had thrown the shells of peanuts which they had eaten. There were the newspapers in which *bondas* were wrapped, also thrown on one side and the wrappers of sweets and chocolates.

"Grandma, look the compartment floor has become so dirty with everyone's waste thrown everywhere," grumbled Gino pointing to the waste he was slipping on, while moving around in the compartment. Before his grandmother could answer a man came sliding around on the floor, with a short handled brush, sweeping up the dirt and collecting it to throw away. In minutes, squatting on his twisted little legs, the man had cleaned the whole compartment up and everyone gave him a coin or two. Gino felt quite grown up to give him a coin too from his pocket money.

"Sadly we do not know how to keep our surroundings clean," said his Grandma. "I agree with you all the *jignut* (peanut) shells could have been put carefully in the newspaper they came in and thrown out in a bin once a station was reached."

As the train clattered along the tracks, Gino sat at the window seat watching the steam engine when the train took a curve and it was visible from his open window.

The steam engine belched great big puffs of black smoke and every once in a while, Gino got a speck of coal in his eye. He liked the smell of the smoke and so much to his grandmother's amusement, he stuck his head against the bars of the window, like she remembered Sabrina, Gino's mother did as a child.

"Be careful that the window does not fall on your fingers Gino," admonished Grandma, as the latches of the windows did not seem to be working well. But as soon as he got a speck which he could not remove, he ran to Grandma who washed his eye out and applied a warm handkerchief on his eye lid, on which she blowed, her sweet smelling breath.

Soon they reached Pune and a whole lot of men got onto the train selling a variety of *chikkie* (peanut brittle). Gino loved *chikkie* and so did Grandma, so it was difficult to choose when there were so many tempting flavours spread out for them by the sellers.

"Choose whatever you like, Grandma," said Gino grandly. "I have plenty of pocket money, which I have been told by Mum to spend."

"Okay, I will take the crushed peanut and the sesame seed variety, one with sugar and one with jaggery," said his Grandmother. She knew that the *chikkie* was around Rs. 5 a small packet and she wanted Gino to feel grown up and spend his own money.

"I will take a few blocks for Mamma as well," said Gino getting really excited thinking of meeting his great-grandmother, whom he had never met before.

Sabrina's grandmother was still fit and healthy in her late sixties or early seventies, at the time. Gino's great grandmother had no shake in her hands and in fact still gave sewing classes in the house. At the time too neither did Sabrina's mother or her father have even the slightest shake in their hands, or even the slightest inkling that in a decade Parkinson's would hit and change their lives forever.

Reading up on the disease from the net, Sabrina learned that there is no one fixed reason for the Parkinsonism. There is an effort to make distinctions between different forms of Parkinson's depending on the cause. Idiopathic Parkinson's is most common, with "idiopathic" meaning that no cause can be found, and that is the worrying reason. Anyone can get it, you or me, as it is not hereditary. Just something in the environment or our food could trigger it.

According to the information given to Sabrina by the doctor they visited, what Parkinson's does is to damage the nerve cells that produce the chemical messenger dopamine. One of dopamine's tasks is to transmit electrical impulses through the nerves from the brain to the muscles. These impulses control our movements. Destruction of the cells reduces the ability to begin or coordinate movements. People who have Parkinson's may therefore have problems with standing straight with the correct balance. That increases the risk of falls and broken bones in these patients.

But the symptoms of Parkinson's can also be the result of other disorders of the nervous system, such as dementia. Infections, tumours and medications like psychotropic drugs can also cause the onset of Parkinson's. On average, according to research, about 1 to 2 out of 1,000 people have Parkinson's. The disease is much more common in older people and around 18 out of 1,000 people over 65 are affected.

The first signs of Parkinson's can become apparent

long before the disease is diagnosed. They are often not noticed at all or are considered to be a normal part of the ageing process. Fine motor skills typically deteriorate and handwriting changes. People sometimes lose their sense of rhythm or their arms no longer swing when walking. Many people's facial expression becomes more fixed. Constipation, difficulty sleeping and mood swings are also common.

Research says, many people experience a deterioration or complete loss of their sense of smell. For Sabrina's Dad it seemed to just destroy everything he could do, in months, but the disease seemed to take longer to hit her Mum and took a few years to destroy her and reduce her to a vegetable, being fed with a pipe attached to her stomach. The reason being Parkinson's had frozen her capacity to swallow and even a spoon or two of water, made her cough uncontrollably as it went down the wrong way.

Reading up on the disease Sabrina learned that it is not unusual for several years to pass between the first signs of the disease and it being actually diagnosed. The course of the disease varies greatly. The symptoms usually come on gradually for some. Over time movements become slower, muscles stiffen and the tremor in the hand becomes more intense. In early stages medication can usually considerably improve symptoms or even make them go away.

After about five to ten years the symptoms often get worse again say doctors. That is because the brain cells are damaged further, as the disease progresses. The effects of the medication are no longer strong enough and fluctuate a lot. The symptoms of the patient alternate between extreme slowness of movement and normal mobility. These are referred to as "off" and "on" phases. The disease can also cause involuntary movements, and people with Parkinson's may occasionally make sudden, jerky motions. Additional symptoms like speech difficulties, poor memory, bladder weakness, hallucinations and depression can occur. Some people like her Mum could also develop dementia with time.

As the disease progressed, Sabrina's parents needed support with all their everyday activities like eating and drinking, standing up and moving about, getting dressed and washing. They found it increasingly difficult to move, and according to research, some people can only speak very quietly or have trouble with just swallowing water, which is the condition Sabrina's mother is in now.

Riding To Pilerne

Their bags packed, Gino and a group of four of his close pals went off to Pilerne in Bardez, a week's holiday in Goa. Sabrina was not too worried as she knew her Dad would keep an eye on the rascally teenagers who were as rambunctious and boisterous as puppies. She was only concerned about them swimming too deep into the ocean, as there were currents in the unfathomable depths, which had claimed tourists lives in her presence, as a youngster. But Gino had been a national level triathlete, so she decided to relax after speaking to the boys. It was time for her to let go those apron strings, tough as it might be.

Getting off at the Panjim bus stop, the boys followed Grandpa to the bus which would take them directly to Marrani, the stop just before the fields leading into the village.

"But Grandpa we would like to hire bikes and they say this bus stop is the best place for a deal," said Gino.

"Oh, okay, let's go and organise bikes for you chaps, I am quite happy riding the bus," said Grandpa as they hitched their back packs higher on their backs and walked towards a man who was renting bikes on the side.

"We want two motorbikes," said Gino to the man in-charge, looking at the bikes all neatly lined up along the pavement. "How much per day?" he asked in Hindi. "Rs. 450 per day and you have to fill the fuel. I need to see your ID, your driver's licence and your address proof," said the man in excellent English.

"Lucky I brought mine," said Michael, Gino's friend and so between them they chose two decent looking bikes after signing the documents and giving their advance. Copies were made of their docs and the originals given back to them. "We will use them for three days and if we are staying on, we will come and renew for another three days," said Gino to the man.

"Give me your bag Grandpa," said Carlos. "We will come to your bus stop, before you can arrive there. Give us the keys of the house so that we have it open for you and aired before you arrive. I will drop Kevin and come back to Marrani for you, just wait there for me," said Carlos sensing his Grandfather's weariness after the overnight bus ride from Bangalore.

The boys hopped onto the bikes and were off, riding with the wind in their hair, over the Mandovi Bridge. "There are two bridges across the Mandovi," shouted Gino to Mickey.

"One of them crashed into the river taking people and cars with it some decades ago."

"Is this the repaired bridge then?" asked Mickey, concern apparent in his voice as their bikes bounced along each rib of the new bridge. "Yes, yes, but now it's fine," says Gino, "look across at the boats all anchored on one side, looks like somewhere in Europe."

The boys looked across at the large expanse of water, a

greenish-blue in the heat of the rising sun. A few fishermen braved the heat, standing on the raised culverts along the bridge, holding on to fishing lines, hoping to snare the odd mullet for lunch. The scent of drying fish pervaded the air around and the white of the paint on the bridge, hurt their eyes.

"We are in Goooaaah!" They shouted excitedly in unison, whooping with excitement, as their bikes headed towards the end of the bridge.

At the end of the bridge, they took the left turn down towards Verem. A huge crowd of cars and bikes clogged the junction and it took a bit of waiting, before they headed downwards. Tree branches from the avenue of trees alongside the road created a canopy above their heads and a cool breeze from the Mandovi River fanned their faces.

"The roads are great," shouted Carlos after having to face the potholes of Bangalore every single day across the city. "Yes, smooth and well-maintained considering the curves and twirls through the buildings. A lot like Portugal we are told."

The deep and reverberating honk of a ships horn across the waters of the Mandovi made them stop to one side, in Verem and stare. A massive ship which looked like a luxury liner was moving across the river and the boys wondered where it was headed.

"Oh, that's the casino," said one of the locals walking down to catch the ferry. "To avoid tax, they have the casino offshore in those fancy-shmancy ships."

The boys looked at one another, making a quick decision to visit the casino at some later date. For now, they looked long and hard, took pictures to send on WhatsApp and

Instagram to their pals but they needed to get to the house, before the bus carrying Grandpa reached.

"Come on guys let's get going or Grandpa might just reach earlier than us," said Gino. "But first, here's a petrol bunk and lets top up with petrol and only then head for the village."

The boys whizzed into the bunk to load up on diesel which to their pleasant surprise was Rs. 20 cheaper than Bangalore. "No wonder tourists love Goa!" said Mickey while asking the attendant to fill up the tank for Rs. 500. The petrol pump was clean and not very crowded, with attendants who smiled for a change, rather than the sullen-faced ones in Bangalore.

The ferry honked loudly in the back ground and the boys after checking the air in their tyres, stopped near the ferry area to watch a couple of cars drive on. "How those drivers manage beats me and I wonder if any car has dropped off the ferry, while trying to drive on," said Carlos to Arun, who was his pillion rider, and they laughed at the thought as they started to move.

Riding through Verem the smell of freshly baking bread just stopped the four of them in their tracks. The little bakery on the main Verem road was a favourite with Gino who sent Carlos off to buy 20 little pois to take home to Pilerne. "Rs. 40 for 20 pois," said the baker, wrapping up two sheets of little hot pois in newspaper for them.

"We had better hurry or we annoy Grandpa if he arrives before us," said Carlos. "I have called Sarathi, our caretaker, to open the house and keep the beds ready. Hopefully the fridge has been turned on with some cold drinking water bottles in it."

Riding on the Goa roads was quite a different experience

from the pot holes of Bangalore. They were smooth like silk winding through the town, or like airport tarmacs which their grandfather called them.

"Woot, woot!" they yelled as the scooters careered across, through the fields into the village.

The fields were a mass of parrot green, lazily waving paddy. The boys shouts could be heard echoing through the bowl of green fields and a flight of slow flying egrets took off into the skies as their scooters raced into the village.

Racing over the little bridge that spanned the creek, the boys shouted out when they saw a few fishermen sitting in the waning sun plying their rods and hoping for a catch.

"We will collect our rods from the house and return to meet you guys," they shouted as they careened towards the house. Soon their scooters took the turn into the village and they excitedly shouted out to Sarathi, who was wheeling his cycle towards the house. His face broke into a wide grin when he saw the boys.

Scrabbling for the keys to open the lock that fastened the gate, he reminded himself to oil the lock later that day, once he opened the house.

"No one is going to get much sleep here," he thought as he looked at the boys excited and happy faces. They have come to shake up the village and in any case the villagers were happy to have the new generation come back, even for a visit.

Role Reversal

Sabrina's sister Samara lived in Chennai and her first baby son was born there. She was working in a big business establishment and did not want to give up her job. She mentioned her predicament to her parents, that she was worried about leaving the new born little baby boy with the hired help. Stories were doing the rounds of how the help would eat up the baby's food and drug them so they were quiet. How sure was she about how the baby would be cared for, while they were at work? Chennai was a new city to which they had moved and quite a different culture and city from Bangalore. A snap decision was made by her Dad—he offered to go to Chennai for a month to help looking after the baby in the house. And the rest of the family took it in turns to go each month to help.

So while Samara dressed hurriedly in her saree, after expressing a few bottles of her own breast milk to feed the child, she pushed the bottles into the fridge and left. It was her Dad who took on the role as a carer of the little, helpless baby and he managed in a small, tiny apartment. Her Dad had to re-learn tying nappies for the baby. How to feed and keep the infant clean and dry and cool in the terrible heat of Chennai. He was physically fine and adored the little baby. A Dad with a heart as big as himself to have done that. While Samara could not have been more grateful, for the gift of safety and health that her Dad had given her baby. Something no money can ever buy.

"Dad, the bottles are in the fridge, just give them to him only at fixed times and if he is still hungry give him a little cerelac," said Samara as she organised all the requirements for the day.

Samara even cooked meals for her Dad and kept them ready for him so he did not have to bother about feeding himself. It was tough but she knew it was such a safe and convenient option, to have family look after the little guy in the house, in familiar surroundings.

A crèche, as they were called, had many other babies as well from all sorts of backgrounds, who could have given the little guy all sorts of germs and infections. Plus cleanliness was ensured at home and of course regular washing and changing of nappies kept his little bottom clear, of any redness and pain.

Now that Sabrina had a role reversal happening in her life, she realised how unselfish her parents had been. They dropped whatever they were doing at the time in their lives and came to support their kids when asked. There was a humility in whatever they did especially her Dad and that is why it was so difficult to accept the complete breakdown which Parkinson's brought in its wake.

Parkinson's turned that serving officer Dad, who was there when she needed him the most, into a man who could not feed himself. He could not grip the spoon, neither could he scoop up the food with the implement. Even if some food got scooped up, the spoon swung wildly around in his hand and he could not guide it to his mouth. Parkinson's had destroyed her strong and seemingly invincible father.

The disease which is a progressive neuron-degenerative illness, has no known cure in sight and so here was a man who had a wonderful career in the armed forces reduced to being washed and fed by the family and the servants, unable to even feed himself.

It was when her father reached his 60s that he began to suffer visibly from Parkinson's which Samara realised is a chronic and progressive movement disorder, meaning that symptoms continue and worsen over time. Millions of people all over the world are living with Parkinson's disease. The cause is unknown, and although there is presently no cure, there are treatment options such as medication and surgery to manage its symptoms.

Sabrina remembered her principal in a school, a brilliant woman who developed a shuffling gait and the terrifying tremor in the hands when she was in her prime. She went to the UK in those days for surgery, which corrected the problem, but sadly she was afflicted all over again. The lady bravely had several operations before she gave up and let the disease take over and she lost her fight with it.

Reading up on the disease Samara realised that Parkinson's involves the malfunction and death of vital nerve cells in the brain, called neurons. It primarily affects neurons in an area of the brain called the substantia nigra. Some of these dying neurons produce dopamine, a chemical that sends messages to the part of the brain that controls movement and coordination. As Parkinson's progresses, the amount of dopamine produced in the brain decreases, leaving a person unable to control movement normally.

The specific group of symptoms that an individual experiences varies from person to person. Online research says that primary motor signs of Parkinson's disease include: tremor of the hands, arms, legs, jaw and face; bradykinesia or slowness of movement; rigidity or stiffness of the limbs and trunk; and postural instability or impaired balance and coordination.

Scientists are also exploring the idea that loss of cells in other areas of the brain and body contribute to Parkinson's. For example, researchers have discovered that the hallmark sign of Parkinson's disease — clumps of a protein alpha-synuclein, which are also called Lewy Bodies — are found not only in the mid-brain but also in the brain stem and the olfactory bulb.

These areas of the brain correlate to non-motor functions, such as sense of smell and sleep regulation. The presence of Lewy bodies in these areas could explain the non-motor symptoms experienced by some people with Parkinson's before any motor sign of the disease appears. The intestines also have dopamine cells that degenerate in Parkinson's, and this may be important in the gastrointestinal symptoms that are part of the disease.

Many years later this gastrointestinal symptom could be seen in her mother who was unable to swallow and feed herself. Finally as she was choking on even the soft foods given to her, a tube was fitted in her stomach and she was manually fed a liquidised mixture of nourishing food poured directly into her stomach via a tube.

The Moore Market

"Oh! Come on lets go shopping after I come back from work," said Samara.

Sabrina had come to Chennai to help Dad babysit Samara's toddler. He was still easily prone to infection and too tiny to be put into a crèche.

"Dad won't mind if we go into town and shop a bit," urged Samara. "So meet me at the bus stop at 5pm and we can hop onto a bus and we can go to Moore Market to browse through the books there."

It was crazily crowded when they got off the bus and walked to Moore Market which is about 1km from the Madras Central station. According to history, Moore Market was originally built to house the hawkers in the Broadway area of Chennai. Its foundation stone was laid by Sir George Moore, president of the Madras Corporation in 1898. The building was designed in the Indo-Saracenic style by RE Ellis and was constructed by A. Subramania Aiyar. The original market, consisted of a series of shops around a central quadrangle, which was finally completed in 1900, and had sections for meat, flowers and food items, but was particularly popular for curios including antiques, art and books. Over the years, it gradually took the status of a flea market where one could buy rare and second hand items for a bargain.

Sadly on 30 May 1985, the market was completely destroyed by a fire, the cause of which still remains an unsolved mystery. The structure was later razed to make way for the new Chennai Suburban Railway terminus and reservation centre. With the demolition of the market and the People's Park, the residents of Chennai were extremely upset and this marked the beginning of heritage activism in the city, which is a relief as many other heritage structures have been saved.

Flower vendors sat outside with their baskets of jasmines, tuber lilies and rose garlands adorned with silver and gold tinsel. Samara and Sabrina gingerly walked through the crowds, stopping once in a while at a book stand to check out the books on sale. Sometimes first editions could be found among the books which probably had belonged to a family, who was getting rid of the stacks of books, which the next generation did not treasure or consider valuable. For a few rupees Sabrina was able to buy an old and yellowed copy of 'Mrs. Dalloway' by Virginia Woolf the British author who committed suicide and her body was recovered from the River Ouse near her weekend house in Lewes in the UK.

'Mrs. Dalloway' was also the name of a quaint book shop that Sabrina frequented while going on work to Berkeley, California. She didn't realise the connection till she read the book. Across the large wall at the back of the shop was painted the first line of the novel, "Mrs. Dalloway said she would buy the flowers herself." She wondered about the line which did not sound fantastically erudite, to gain such notoriety, till she learned that Woolf had been born into a wealthy family in Kensington and her fame spread as she was considered a pioneer of feminist texts.

Samara scoured the market for pickles and local snacks that her father enjoyed and both sisters curiously looked at the range of *kanchi* cotton *sarees* on display. The variety and colours made it difficult for them to choose.

"How does this Peacock blue with a magenta border look?" asked Samara fingering a dressy looking *Kanchipuram* cotton.

"The asking price is Rs 1,500 which is fairly steep but I love the colours. Let's see if we can bargain with him for a more reasonable price," said Samara.

"Stop looking like you will die if you don't get it, or the price won't come down," said Sabrina.

"In Chennai, you have to suggest a price closer to half and then start walking away," said Samara.

"Okay, if you can cut the price, I would like to buy the chequered yellow one with the purple border," said Sabrina who loved cotton *sarees.*

"Remember most people in Madras speak English, so watch what you say," said Samara.

So the haggling on the price began, but the shop keeper seemed to be winning this round when Samara seemed to tire and decide to walk away.

"Final price Madam?" shouted the shopkeeper cheekily.

"Okay, Rs. 1000," said Samara, but the shopkeeper shook his head and said, "Give me a better price and I can see if it works for me."

"I can't go beyond Rs. 1100," and they looked expectantly at the shopkeeper who smiled widely and agreed. His smile grew even wider when he realised Sabrina too was keen on settling for another *saree* for herself.

Gathering up their treasures made sweeter with the bargain they made, the sisters decided to take the bus home to Kilpauk where Samara lived. They made their way through the jostling crowd, when suddenly Sabrina heard Samara squeal in pain and in a flash kick off her slipper, pick it up and go after a man in the crowd.

"Pinched me, did you? How dare you pinch me? Would you like it if a stranger pinched your sister or your mother?" *Whack, whack, whack* went Samara, hitting out at the man who obviously did not expect this reaction. Samara was dressed in her striking airline *saree* and she wore her *saree* with much panache on her hips. She had a great figure but she had never been accosted by any man in that fashion before in Chennai, though she travelled by bus every day .

Sabrina stood along with her in shock, ready to fly to her defence, if there were repercussions, but instead the man began to plead for mercy, when he saw an annoyed crowd gather around him. Obviously this eve-teaser had got away with quiet responses when he groped women before. He definitely did not expect to be exposed in this fashion and it was good to see a supportive crowd.

Sabrina took a couple of deep breaths and steadied herself. Then pulled Samara away saying, "Let's get out of here now that it's getting dark and we could get accosted by a group."

They both ran to the bus stop and to Samara's relief, the bus to take them home to Kilpauk arrived in minutes and they jumped on. Once they paid the conductor for their tickets the enormity of what had happened sank in and Sabrina started giggling, Samara's rage dissipated and she began to giggle too. Their giggles turned to guffaws and they tried desperately to keep it down, tears of laughter streaming down their faces, while other passengers looked at them curiously.

Once they reached home they told their father about their encounter. Dad was not happy. "Never try something like that again, especially when you're on your own," he admonished. "It's safer to have a man along with you to intervene, in case it gets ugly and they retaliate."

Samara's husband too was shocked and horrified and advised both sisters to be cautious when alone. "If one of us men were with you that's fine, but don't try it on your own again, it's dangerous and the man can turn around and get nasty."

Then they sat down to have a hot cup of tea, which their Dad poured into mugs with an absolutely steady hand. There was no tremor at all in either of his hands, though sometimes the girls noticed the page of the newspaper he was reading quiver, but they never gave it another thought.

The girls then sat back to recount the incident once again to their Dad, while they fell about laughing, remembering the man's shocked face and the crowd of curious onlookers who were on their side.

The Sound Of Children

Once her mother retired from working in one of the more famous schools in the city, she decided to build her own pre-school at the back of the house. Sabrina's mother had never taught very young children in any of her previous positions so this was an absolutely new and novel experience. She was more accustomed to teaching teenagers difficult subjects like Literature and Geography.

So again, running her pre-school meant she delved into her capacity as a grandmother and her interaction with her own grandchildren, and used that as experience. The school was called 'The ABC Academy', a name Sabrina had suggested when she was trying to decide upon a name for her pre-school.

It was exciting to see the school name board being designed in black and white and the lettering being planned by the designer. The school furniture too was professionally designed as were the pictures on the walls painstakingly chosen and framed. The building was brand new with a large hall for the main school area and the principal's office, in which her mother hardly ever got a chance to relax in. Large windows were inserted to let the fresh air in, and the old trees of the homestead literally encased the school building, in their arms.

Around the play area grew an old *chikoo* tree, which had been probably planted in her Grandfather's time. Great big oval *chikoos* grew on the tree and it had several crops in a year. The tree now grew around the children's sand pit, where the kids built sand castles and were allowed to scrabble around, in the lovely golden coloured sand, which her mother especially ordered. Old empty tins and plastic glasses were given to the kids to play with in the sand, building sand castles and moats.

A see-saw and slide too gave them much joy and there was a lot of noise and laughter every day when it was play time for the kids. The neighbour's purple Jacaranda blossom showered down on the kids play area, as the tree was alongside the property wall. The dainty purple trumpet shaped blooms, made a carpet on the sandpit and around the play area giving the children another bit of nature to enjoy.

Every few months Sabrina's mother asked her Dad to harvest the *chikoos* which grew like a rash on the tree. The tree being large gave at least 250 fruits per crop.

"The tree is happy, that's why it is fruiting," said her father.

"Trees love noise and the sound of children's voices. That is why this tree which had stopped fruiting when you all grew up and left, is now happy and fruiting copiously again," said her father sagely. It seemed true enough as they had not put any compost to the tree and neither had the base been dug up and the soil loosened around it's roots.

"Bring the cloth bag from the hook in the kitchen, Sabrina," shouted her Dad and along with the babies watching, he picked a large *chikoo*, rubbed the oozing 'milk' that came out when it was freshly picked into the mud and popped it into the bag.

"Don't let any of the kids pick the fruit," instructed her Mum, "because the *dik* can be harmful for their eyes."

Sabrina and her father picked almost 75 fruits before they stopped, quite tired with the exertion. All the little kids were given half a dozen each to take home, when their parents came to fetch them.

"Let them ripen in a carton or among some crushed newspapers," advised her Dad and all the kids went happily home with their fruity haul.

"We will pick another load once they grow bigger, after two weeks," said her Dad, wiping his sticky hands in some sand to get the *dik* (sticky white milky substance) off them.

"Rub your hands in the sand, that will take off the worst of the stickiness Sabrina," said her Dad.

"Then come and use this cake of Lifebuoy soap, to take off the balance which is difficult to get at in-between the fingers."

Rather than waste the water used to wash his hands down the drain, Sabrina's Dad asked her to pour a mug over his hands, as he washed them at the base of the Bottle brush tree. That is when Sabrina noticed a strange tremor in her father's fingers. As he washed his hands his fingers shivered peculiarly and slipped as he tried to grip his palms together, to wash them. However Sabrina did not pay too much attention to it at that moment, it was only later she realised that the tremors of Parkinson's had begun in her Dad in his sixties, when he had just retired from the services. Her mother seemed to be fine and did not have any sort of tremors at all in her body as yet.

Reading up on the issue, Sabrina learned that a resting tremor is often the first symptom of the disorder, and occurs in approximately 70% of the victims. The tremor is generally asymmetric and increases with anxiety and certain types of motor activity and when walking. The resting tremor most appears first in the hands in the majority of cases, although there are some cases in which it first appears in the feet.

Bradykinesia is the most disabling symptom of the disease, and has the heaviest impact on fine motor movements such as writing. Her Dad was already finding it difficult to sign cheques and write letters. Most often he called Sabrina to sit at the table and take a dictation, to which he affixed a scrawled signature. When Samara was in town visiting from the Middle East, she too was asked to come and take a dictation, which was rather a strange request, from a Dad who normally did all his own work, independently.

Parkinson's also tends to reduce arm movements while walking and that is what she noticed with her father when he went walking to the market, bag slung on his shoulder. He had stopped riding his scooter as the grip in his hands had reduced noticeably and that scared him though he did not verbalise it.

There was the beginnings of postural instability in her father as well, which in more advanced cases, is manifested by decreasing ability to maintain balance, leading to increased risk of falling and collateral harm caused by the fall, like the breaking of limbs. He was a cautious man and realising that he could fall on the road, he only walked small distances, on known paths.

Postural instability is generally an indication of relatively advanced Parkinson's Disease, says research, with the gait of the person becoming slower, as the victim has more difficulty maintaining the required level of coordination to walk and stand erect. At this time, Sabrina remembered her Grandfather and his advanced postural instability, where he needed to be helped with all he did.

However the fact that her grandfather and her father had the disease made Sabrina wonder if the disease was hereditary at all. But then again there is no definite research to prove that it is.

Signs Of Change

The signs of Parkinson's can be very different in different people. In Sabrina's Dad, the signs were rather early in his retired life and very marked. He stiffened in his gait and his entire body sloped forwards after his mid 60s. That was shocking for Sabrina's family as he had been a very active sportsman, right till the time he retired from the Indian Air Force. Sabrina still had memories of him taking his curved hockey stick to work for a game, which was played while he was heading the division, just before he retired. In fact he rode the scooter to Jalahalli to the end, something she shudders to think of today. His hand did shake as he gripped the handle-bars she remembered, but he did not let it bother him. He kept riding the scooter to-and-fro till the day he retired.

For her Mother, the slowed movement and visible shake only appeared, when she needed to write and much later in her 70s. In fact the doctors were so shocked to realise that they were husband and wife who both had the disease, which was a rather uncommon occurrence.

"Are you saying your Dad had Parkinson's as well?" asked the doctor in shock when Sabrina took her Mum for a check-up once to a new physician. Her Dad always wanted to go to his doctor in the Military Hospital. Mum preferred going to the Manipal Hospital and later to Fortis, as she felt the doctors there were better equipped to help her.

"I will decrease her dopamine," the doctor told Sabrina, "as she is wheel-chair bound and so does not need as much for her walking movement." But slowly the disease robbed her mother of the ability to sign and Sabrina would squirm, when she had to take her thumb impression, when beginning work on the family building, on Castle Street, in the city.

"What must she feel?" Sabrina often wondered when strange men from the Corporation arrived to take her thumb impression on documents. She sat stiff with no facial expression, while the secretary pressed her thumb on the ink pad and affixed it to the document. A woman who had done her Masters when she was in her early 50s reduced to this? It broke Sabrina's heart to see it.

Reading up about the disease, on the US National Library of Medicine the typical symptoms which corroborated with Sabrina's parents connected the dots.

Slowed movement (akinesia): Movements can only be performed slowly. Affected people might walk very hesitantly and only take short, increasingly small steps. They find it hard to start moving – taking the first step is often particularly difficult. Once they are moving, it becomes increasingly difficult to stop again, for example to stand still on command. As the disease progresses, the arms stop swinging when walking and they look like automation shuffling around.

Gripping with the hands and tasks that require a certain degree of dexterity like tying shoelaces also become more difficult. Due to reduced activity in the facial muscles, the face becomes more and more mask-like and that could be seen in both Sabrina's parents. Both such good looking people in their younger days had turned literally to stone, without much facial expression at all. Their speech too became quiet and monotone and over time swallowing also became impossible.

In fact, since Sabrina's Mum outlived her Dad and has had the disease for longer, she is now unable to swallow at all and the doctors have affixed a tube to her stomach to feed her. She would cough and choke and sometimes specks of food would go down the wrong way, causing great distress. Today even a sip of water has to be given very carefully to her as she is unable to comprehend why she is not being fed and her complaint when she sees Sabrina or Samara is "they are starving me and giving me no food". She is unable to internalise that her feeding is direct through the walls of the stomach.

Muscle stiffness (rigidity): Especially the arms, legs and neck can become stiff and tense. Even if somebody else tries to move the person's arms and legs, the muscles usually put up resistance or cannot be moved at all, and stiffen up even more during such attempts. This excessive tensing of the muscles often causes aches. This is what Sabrina's mother has to endure everyday. When she is bathed or moved from the bed to the chair and back. Sadly she cries out when the physiotherapist exercises her every other day. Only now while researching this book Sabrina could understand, why her mother cries out in pain and why it is painful for her to hear it.

Tremor at rest: Most people with Parkinson's have a tremor. It decreases during movement of the hand. It is particularly visible in the hands and that causes people's handwriting to become smaller and less clear. The mind is still clear, the body can still move, but the hands do not obey the mind.

Sabrina would take her Dad and Mum to parties and weddings and she hated to see the pity in people's eyes when they saw her feeding her father his meal. It angered her because her Dad was a strong man reduced to this helpless situation, due to the disease. Sabrina had to break up the chicken or the *vada* which her father loved to eat and putting the spoon with food into his mouth was so difficult for her to do, without feeling intense pain. He had probably done it to her as a little girl and Sabrina cried when she thought about it later.

Possible other effects of Parkinson's included bladder and digestion disorders, circulation problems, difficulties in concentrating, and depression. The latter she saw very pronounced in her father who slept for hours probably to escape from feeling helpless. He was not the man on the go that she remembered any more. Instead he spent a lot of time in the bedroom, only coming out for his meals when called.

Everyday Triggers

Over the years, sadly the ravages of memory loss with Parkinson's overtook both Sabrina's parents. No one ever accepts, that it is the use of various drugs and lifestyle changes, which brings in Parkinson's into many seniors' lives. There was one incident that Sabrina remembered clearly when a doctor relative warned of the use of aluminium *dekchis* (cooking utensils) and other utensils when cooking. "You scrape the *dekchi* while cooking and when emptying it of the food, the *dekchi* is scraped off some of its aluminium, which is swallowed by us when eating the meal."

"As long as we used mud pots there was no side effect, if we ate any of the mud that came off the pot. Mud has no side effects, but aluminium we all are aware today of its negative effects."

Today there are a lot of simple lifestyle changes which can literally save your life—natural therapies to prevent and avoid these degenerative diseases. We do not have to allow our minds to degenerate as we age. We do not have to allow ourselves to turn into vegetables and become totally dependent on kids, who might not want to look after us. And how many of us want to be reduced to living sad lives in homes for the aged? After all, old age will hit all of us someday.

There are simple things to do to try and prevent us from contracting Parkinson's of which there is no cure, as of now. Everyone over the age of 40 needs to be concerned about these disorders which are destroying so many of our senior citizens. The disease may take decades to develop and most of us rarely show symptoms of the disease, in the early stages. Unfortunately people with brain damage do not know till it's too late and the disease has already taken hold of the nervous system.

There are specific reasons that people develop the disease. They could be anything from dietary deficiencies, toxins in the environment, like for example the modern method of fogging or sleeping with a mosquito repellent on through the night, that we inhale too. There could be harmful ingredients in everyday foods like preservatives in pickles and jams and even tinned food that many of us love.

What about everyday household products, we might ask. Sprays and air fresheners all contain chemicals which we happily purchase and breathe in. Insecticides which we spray without a second thought into our cupboards, especially where cockroaches multiply. The spray can settle on open food or food which are inside open bags. We have to be careful while using them, covering our faces and noses with masks, if we still need to use them. Parkinson's takes decades to develop and we don't know we are suffering from it, until it's upon us.

Sabrina's Dad was a robust energetic man, an athlete, a champion who cleared the decks of medals and cups during college and school sports tournaments. He turned into a weak, emaciated shadow of himself, too shaky and frail to even feed himself. He spent most of his days lying in bed, or sitting in the verandah looking out into the garden with unseeing eyes. It was emotionally wrenching for Sabrina to watch her father die in such pain. The doctors refused to let him have anything sweet to eat as he was diabetic and he longed for *Nagpuri* oranges and Cheese Twists from a bakery called *Durga's*.

Sabrina lived the nightmare along with him, peeling the orange pods and letting him enjoy them, right in the hospital. Giving him the cheese twists, which he ate with child-like joy. Conventional medicines had failed her Dad and it's sad that today there are still no curative discoveries on the horizon. His slow and painful death had a profound effect, of sorrow and bereavement for the whole family especially her mother. It was obvious that medical treatments could not help them. And Sabrina hoped that natural solutions should help doctors and researchers get to the root cause.

Why have conventional methods failed, she asked herself over and over again. They have failed because we humans are not concerned about the underlying causes or cures. Our conventional medical system is based on drug therapies. And what is drug therapy meant to do? Drug therapy is meant to treat symptoms and not to cure. Conventional methods includes ongoing treatment for life. A patient is hooked onto taking drugs for life and hoping to alleviate the symptoms.

Parkinson's disease destroys our brain and we need to fight back, and save and protect it to maintain our memory. So doctors have looked at the causes and solutions. Memory loss is primarily caused by two things—inflammation and free radical damage. Get these culprits under control and drastically reduce your risk. There are specific triggers and we can neutralize them. Each brain cell is like a little factory which produces energy, enzymes and proteins.

Free radicals damage the brain cells which eventually fail and die. Free radicals are highly reactive, sub-microscopic particles. Like water dripping on a stone slowly wearing it away. Open to triggers causes it. Free radicals kill your cells or your brain. Initially the effects are very small and not noticeable, like water dripping on stone. This is because antioxidant defences decline with age and humans lose triggers which overwhelm antioxidants. From the age of 50 to 60 onwards, our defences start declining rapidly. With this there is an escalation of free radicals. What is frightening is that today, the average age of onset of Parkinson's has dropped to 57, while memory loss is normal with ageing.

Scientists say that the triggers that cause Parkinson's are, a variety of pesticides and herbicides, sugars and sugar substitutes, harmful ingredients in food and beverages, toxic metals in air, water, consumer products, omega 6 fats, nutritional deficiencies, vaccines, lack of exercise and hormonal imbalances. Parkinson's caused by brain inflammation happens, when the brain's immune cells overreact and destroys the midsection of brain.

Parkinson's Disease is the most common serious movement disorder in the world, affecting approximately 1% of the adult population over the age of 60. The disease is the result of progressive loss of neurons in substantia nigra portion of the brain, which produces the general symptoms of tremors. The symptoms can be controlled by a drug regimen with a surgical intervention as an option for patients that no longer respond to drug therapy.

There is recent evidence that the disease may be genetic in nature, with duplication of the alpha-synuclein gene linked to the onset of Parkinson's Disease, its severity and progression. The disorder is named after the physician, James Parkinson, who described its symptoms in an 1817 monograph entitled, "An Essay on the Shaking Palsy."

According to details of the disease, Parkinson's Disease, describes a syndrome that is characterized by both tremors and rigidity, and is usually asymmetric in that it affects one side of the body more than the other. Symptoms also include bradykinesia, which is slowed ability to start and continue movements and adjust the body's position. Although motor dysfunction defines the disorder, it also involves other symptoms such as cognitive or psychiatric changes and sleep disturbances.

"It is generally responsive to a dopamine treatment, which may be due to the fact that the disease produces the deterioration of the nigral dopamine neurons during the progression of the disease," advised the doctor who looked after her mother and increased or decreased the medication according to her mother's condition.

The onset of the disease in the majority of cases occurs around the age of 60, although there are cases of younger onset and even cases of juvenile onset. The age of onset often impacts the way in which symptoms develop, with younger victims less likely to experience postural instability.

Nail In The Coffin

Sabrina and Samara could see their father becoming weaker and less independent as the years went by. He would force himself to take a bus and go to Goa but after a while he stopped as he found making the trip difficult. In fact the boys felt that their grandfather was losing his sight as well, but he tried to hide it. The only indication that he was having any trouble seeing was when suddenly he started wearing a pair of spectacles.

"Can I get you the newspaper to read out there in the verandah Grandpa?" asked Gino when he had visited one day and found his grandfather sitting quietly in the front verandah, just staring into space.

"Yes, sure!" said his Grandpa, but in a few minutes Gino had noticed him sitting quietly again, with the newspaper folded to one side. He obviously did not want to show anyone that he could not hold up the newspaper to read. His hands shook so uncontrollably he was unable to hold it up, let alone read it.

His Grandpa used to enjoy going out into the school room too and helping with the children. He had stopped doing that, preferring to stay indoors in the house.

"Why don't you come sit out here with the kids?" called her mother. "It's snack time and they are all going to sit out in the sun and enjoy their snack and some juice. You can have your cup of tea with them."

But there was no reply from her father, whose movements too, had begun to slow down considerably. Her father's leather slippers which he always bought from Goa and kept a supply in the house, would scrape along the floor as he walked to the toilet, or went to lie down in the bed. His arms hung limply along the sides of his body, as he shuffled around increasingly and took over his movements, typical of the Parkinson's disease.

Researching on the disease, Sabrina found that cognitive and psychiatric symptoms also develop in advanced Parkinson's Disease, with studies indicating that between 40% and 80% of the victims develop dementia in the end stage of the disease. In some individuals, the dementia and the drugs used to treat the disorder can lead to hallucinations and other types of psychotic behaviours. This happened with her father, but was put down to PTS (Post Traumatic Stress) which he faced when he was called out to the 1971 war.

Disturbed sleep is also common in the disorder, with symptoms such as depression and restless leg syndrome impacting the ability of the victim to sleep. In many cases, there is also involvement of the autonomic nervous system that leads to constipation or urinary urgency. Since her father also suffered from advanced and chronic diabetes, these symptoms were attributed to diabetes too and not Parkinson's.

Reading up studies on Parkinson's, one realises that there is no definitive test for diagnosing Parkinson's

Disease. The diagnosis is based on the collection of symptoms, displayed by the patient that fit the criteria for the disease. In some cases, it is difficult to separate the symptoms of normal ageing from those of the disease, with asymmetric tremors used more often to confirm the diagnosis. In addition, other types of diseases result in the individual displaying symptoms similar to Parkinson's Disease.

As a result, the confirmed diagnosis of Parkinson's disease can be delayed in some cases. In some situations, a diagnosis of Parkinson's can be confirmed based on the response of the patient to medications. There are also situations in which the symptoms of the disease are induced by the patient taking a certain type of drug. In these cases the patient is not suffering from Parkinson's Disease, but rather from a collection of symptoms described as Parkinsonism that are similar to the symptoms of the disorder. In most cases, the symptoms abate once the drug is discontinued.

The cause of the symptoms associated with Parkinson's Disease is the depletion of dopamine produced by the brain due to degeneration of the nerve cells that produce the chemical. Dopamine is a neurotransmitter that stimulates motor neurons, which are the nerve cells that control muscles. By the time that symptoms appear, victims of the disorder have lost 80% or more of their dopamine production capabilities. There is no cure for this condition, with treatment focusing on medications to control symptoms and a surgical intervention in more extreme cases.

For Sabrina's mother, the drug Levodopa is the primary medication used to treat symptoms and is based on a strategy of dopamine replacement. The drug is converted into dopamine by an enzyme in the brain. There are other drugs that use different strategies to combat the disorder, but all of the treatments have a high potential for substantial side effects. In addition, the drug treatments tend to lose effectiveness over time as the disease progresses and the body develops resistance to the drugs.

When medications become ineffective in controlling symptoms or the side effects are severe, surgery may be used to control the symptoms of the disease. Only 10% of the individuals with Parkinson's disease can undergo surgery because of the variety of criteria that are used, to screen patients for the somewhat risky procedures.

Information gleaned from medical websites explain that ablative surgery consists of destroying the brain tissue that is producing the abnormal chemicals that result in symptoms. This is done by various methods, such as the use of an electric probe used in the procedure. It is very difficult to estimate the amount of tissue that should be destroyed, increasing the risk that healthy tissue will also be destroyed.

Another method used is Deep Brain Stimulation, which is a surgical method that implants an electrode in the brain that temporarily deactivates the activity of the tissue in the area surrounding the electrode. There is a risk that the implant can become infected and so is not used in diabetics like Sabrina's mother.

A third surgical technique is restorative in nature through transplanting dopamine producing cells into the brain, which are intended to replace the functioning of the cells damaged by the disorder. The source of the cells that are transplanted is important to the success rate, with 90% of foetal transplant cells failing to survive, while preliminary studies at this time suggest that pig embryo cells may have a better chance of survival. While the mechanism that produces the symptoms is understood, the reasons behind the degeneration of the dopamine-producing nerve cells in the brain remain somewhat unclear.

None of the procedures could be even considered for Sabrina's father as he was severely diabetic and the doctors were unwilling to let him go under the knife, as chances of successful recovery was slim. In fact for the final hospitalization of her father in the Military Hospital, he was exceedingly weak and barely coherent.

"Dad, you have a really nice room here in the hospital," said Sabrina, looking around the lovely, airy room he had been given as a senior officer, but he barely noticed his surroundings.

"What's this fallen under the bed?" she asked trying to move a small brown dry object with her shoe. Picking it up a feeling of fear and revulsion just swamped her when she realised it was one of her father's toes, which had just fallen off his foot.

A combination of Parkinson's and Diabetes drove the final nail into her father's coffin.

The Old Age Home

After Sabrina and Samara's father died, their mother enjoyed living in the huge and rambling house on her own. The only problem was she had fallen down while on holiday in Goa and in spite of an operation, was unable to walk on her own. She tried using a walker but it did not help her back on her feet in fact after a while because of being seated in her wheel chair all the time, her legs began to atrophy. Because she was dependant so heavily on the servants they began to take advantage and not arrive to work, very often making it impossible for her to manage on her own.

"Will you come and spend the night with me, Sabrina?" was the call Sabrina would get every once in a while. "Devika has not shown up and she called to say her husband was unwell and so was not coming in."

That meant leaving the little boys on their own with their Dad and driving down in the dark, to spend the night with her mother. Yes there was a dog, which was pretty fierce and kept intruders at bay, but the papers were full of old people being murdered in their beds, for nothing worth stealing, by petty thieves. They found breaking into these old colonial homes easy, either by lifting the tiles from the roof and lowering themselves in, or just forcing the open weak toilet doors. When the murders came too close to comfort to Convent Road, her mother began worrying and thinking about going away, to live in an old age home.

The concept was becoming popular in the city at the time and Sabrina's mother began looking around at various homes, but she never really made up her mind. Sabrina felt that she was unsure of how she would fit in, into the home. Would she have company, would she be happy there worried her a lot and made her indecisive. However the fact that she was vulnerable, because she was immobile was her greatest fear and coloured all that she wanted to do.

"I have been talking to friends who have moved to a home and they are managing very well there, making new friends," said her Mum suddenly one morning when Devika did not arrive. "I even asked them if I could take some of my furniture to the home and they agreed and promised to give me a very large room where even my dining table can fit. I can have my own fridge in as well," she said happily.

"Ah ha! So you can have big blocks of ice-cream in the freezer and eat it for breakfast, lunch and dinner?" teased Sabrina.

Her mother loved ice-cream and could eat large helpings of the plain vanilla flavour, dunked in chocolate sauce. She also enjoyed the special Rum and Raisin flavour and did not need a special occasion to ask for a bowl of it.

"Look the room is nice and large," said her Mum. "And I have been able to bring in the dining table and the sofa set," said her mother showing her the room she had moved into.

"Yes, I can see that," said Sabrina, sitting down on the sofa that creaked embarrassingly, like it had always done in the old house.

A big cage of budgerigars twittered and squawked at the end of the verandah and the garden outside was lush and green. Sprawling manicured lawns spread over the front of the rooms with their inmates, and at first their mother seemed happy in her new surroundings. However, soon the cracks began to show and the first problem which was insurmountable, was the food served to their mother. It was too heavily spiced and she could not tolerate eating mostly vegetarian fare, every single day.

Sabrina noticed that her mother was slowly retreating into herself and the shake in her hands were getting more pronounced. Her speech, too, was becoming difficult and she had to be fed her food as the tremor was strong. She could not even stir her cup of coffee and that had become very difficult for her to bear. Visiting her one Sunday, Sabrina found her in tears and extremely agitated.

"When is the building going to be ready? Last night some people came into my room and slept on my bed. They even had a party and ate up all my ice-cream."

It was a terribly difficult time for Sabrina, who could not imagine that her clever and capable mother, was bordering on dementia. Every time they visited she would tell them stories, which made no sense and the worst blow was when she complained of ill-treatment by the servants. Were they the hallucinations that the doctor told her to expect with the progression of Parkinson's or was it for real, wondered Sabrina.

"They pinch me and slap me while I bathe," she said, her face full of pain and sorrow. No matter how much Sabrina tried to verify the situation, and called the administrators to listen to her complaints, her mother never went back on what she said. Sabrina could see her mother deteriorate in front of her eyes, and there was nothing she could do. Often when she visited the home she would see her just sitting quietly inside the room in her chair, with no one for company. Sadly, over time, dementia seemed to be taking over the once sprightly woman and reducing her into a complaining old woman.

A combination of Parkinson's and dementia had seized her and by the end of five years, it seemed like she was heading for sure death. The building where her home once was, took five years to complete and by then she had lost her will to live. And unfortunately with her diabetes, the doctors could not try any invasive treatment.

"We cannot open up her brain and put in an electrode for Deep Brain Stimulation (DBS)," explained the doctor to Sabrina at one of her umpteen visits with her mother to the specialist. "Diabetic patients are high-risk and we cannot take a chance with your mother. She is not an ideal candidate and could die of complications if we open up her brain."

Reading up on the Parkinson's Foundation website one learns about the facts about the procedure. Deep Brain Stimulation (DBS) is a surgical procedure used to treat a variety of disabling neurological symptoms—most commonly the debilitating symptoms of Parkinson's disease (PD), such as tremor, rigidity, stiffness, slowed movement, and walking problems.

The procedure is also used to treat essential tremor, a common neurological movement disorder. DBS does not damage healthy brain tissue by destroying nerve cells. Instead the procedure blocks electrical signals from targeted areas in the brain.

At present, the procedure is used only for patients whose symptoms cannot be adequately controlled with medications. DBS uses a surgically implanted, battery-operated medical device called a neurostimulator—similar to a heart pacemaker and approximately the size of a stopwatch—to deliver electrical stimulation to targeted areas in the brain that control movement, blocking the abnormal nerve signals that cause tremor and PD symptoms. Some surgeons may use micro-electrode recording—which involves a small wire that monitors the activity of nerve cells in the target area—to more specifically identify the precise brain target that will be stimulated.

Once the system is in place, electrical impulses are sent from the neurostimulator up along the extension wire and the lead and into the brain. These impulses interfere with and block the electrical signals that cause PD symptoms.

The DBS system consists of three components:

1. The lead (also called an electrode) is a thin, insulated wire that is inserted through a small opening in the skull and implanted in the brain. The tip of the electrode is positioned within the targeted brain area.

2. The extension is an insulated wire that is passed under the skin of the head, neck, and shoulder, connecting the lead to the neurostimulator.

3. The neurostimulator (the battery pack) is the third component and is usually implanted under the skin near the collarbone. In some cases it may be implanted lower in the chest or under the skin over the abdomen.

There are three brain targets that have been FDA

approved in the US, for use in Parkinson's disease.

Target choice should be tailored to a patient's individual needs (Benabid, Benazzouz et al. 1998; Okun and Vitek 2004; Benabid, Chabardes et al. 2005; Rodriguez, Fernandez et al. 2007).

There are many ongoing studies that will help to refine target choice for individual patients.

A Living Skeleton

Once the building was complete, Sabrina's mother was brought "home" to Hayes Road and the sisters hoped she would get better, now that she was back on familiar ground. She had left behind the old age home, where she had been terribly unhappy and the distance from her daughters had compounded her loneliness and grief. Sabrina and Samara hoped that coming home would make a difference to her condition and could transform her mind exponentially.

One could only imagine the trauma and tragic shock the sisters experienced, to hear her make just made one damning statement on her return, in a flat and emotionless voice, "This is not Hayes Road, take me back to Hayes Road." Sabrina felt the tears streaming down her face when she realised her mother was unable to comprehend that the old homestead was not there any more. The new and glitzy apartment block to her, was not the Hayes Road she remembered and loved.

The whole place was completely different and did not look like the old colonial bungalow that she had entered as a young bride. The untidy garden full of fruit trees and birds had been replaced by a manicured lawn with prim and proper beds, filled with expensive flowering plants, which the old home did not have. It had a motley collection of orchids and dozens of pots around the house, not this new and different garden, so unlike the old.

But, sadly, nothing grew with gay abandon like it did in the old home, because the five floor structure cut out most of the sunlight. Plants were put down and replanted once they died to no avail over the years. Only the garden on the terrace grew and flowered in the life giving sunlight.

Sabrina felt her Mum regress further still. Like the plants in the garden, she did not feel comfortable in her new surroundings and the disease took hold of her throat muscles. She would cough uncontrollably if given water or tea to swallow and her food became a pulverized, squishy, kiddy meal, served minimally. This was the ultimate test for their mother who enjoyed good food and was reduced to swallowing a mushy mess to live.

After a particularly bad bout of pneumonia, where she was rushed to the hospital to clear her chest inflammation, the doctors suggested placing a tube in her stomach through which liquid food could be poured down. Specks of food could be the cause of the inflammation, they said. It was terrible for Sabrina or Samara to face their mother, who demanded why she was not being fed. She tasted no food on her tongue and that meant she was not fed.

It was disturbing and heart rending for them to explain to her that she could not swallow any more and so she was being fed through the tube. They were unsure if she even understood what she was being told to her about her condition, because she did not seem to recognise them either.

Slowly, the flesh from her bones fell away and, Sabrina

and Samara were mute witnesses of all that was left of her. Literally a living skeleton of their beloved, fashionable and highly-qualified mother. A skeleton who has to be given physiotherapy every other day, to keep her from freezing over completely. She is still given a mash-up of her medicines in her meal, to keep her going, but it is extremely hard for the carer to see what she has been reduced to.

Servants have been employed, being paid large sums to look after her day and night. All the girls' parents' savings made in the hope of travelling the world, go in paying these servants to care for her and to provide them meals. It is a slow torture for her and one wonders what is in store for her everyday. In fact Sabrina prays, hoping she will pass painlessly, as she has suffered more than any human should. She has a strong heart however, that keeps her going day after day and sadly her quality of life, to which the disease has reduced her, is not something which should be wished on anyone.

Nobody can predict the future. Sabrina's parents could not, they never knew what life had in store for them. "You just have to give life your all" was the expression they used at home and the one they lived by. The sisters Sabrina and Samara were taught to be true to their family. And by that adage, they had to do their best to take care of the parents who nurtured them, giving them every last drop of love they had.

This book chronicles the decline which perfectly healthy humans can descend into. Parkinson's is not a disease to be taken lightly and the main lesson that can be taken from this book is—'From caring comes courage, the courage to love and the courage to care in spite of it all. Care for that parent because in seconds they can be reduced to losing all cognitive powers and you have lost the power to say just a simple "Hi Mum!" or "Hi Dad!" forever.'

About Parkinson's

Anyone with a loved one with Parkinson's, should read through this chapter to give themselves a better understanding of the dreaded disease. The slow onset of the disease gives one time to accept and understand that there is no reversal, but medication can slow it down. This gives you breathing time to enjoy what remaining time is left with the patient before they get overwhelmed by the disease.

Every living organism contains genetic material, including animals, people, plants and bacteria. According to the Human Genome Organization, the human genetic code is a complex production of proteins. With regard to the complexity of the human being, it is likely that humans are vastly different in minor ways. So, in a crowd, there are typically no two individuals who look exactly alike or think alike. But at the same time, all of the individuals are functioning basically in the same way, with their lungs breathing and their hearts beating. And except for individuals who have deformities or who have experienced accidents, human beings will all have, two eyes, two ears, a nose, and a mouth, and five senses.

According to many peer-reviewed papers and information on medical sites on the net, there appears to be some genetic causes to Parkinson's Disease, with studies showing that it does tend to run in families. Recently, a team of researchers has determined that the duplication of the alpha-synuclein gene may be the causative factor for the disease, with a genetic link to the duplication. The findings of this study suggest that there is a direct relationship between the amount of alpha-synuclein that the body produces and the age of onset of Parkinson's

Disease, its severity and its rate of progression.

Other studies have linked point mutation in the gene in the development of familial forms of the disorder. In addition, individuals with triplication of the alpha-synuclein gene have a very early onset of the disorder and uncommonly severe symptoms. While the identification of a genetic link that is causative of the disorder can be of assistance in diagnosis of the disease, through more refined diagnostic testing, it does not currently provide assistance with the treatment of the disease.

In the future, however, scientists hope there may be some type of preventive drug regimen, could potential reduce the negative impact, of the over production of alpha-synuclein on the dopamine producing cells of the brain, with screening for the genetic factor determining whether such an approach is required. At the current time, however, the use of genetic screening and potential methods to inhibit the development of the disease remain speculative. In a sense, the notion of complexity is dependent upon the exact question being raised.

Fortunately say scientists, the specie of human is not so complex that the notion of a map of the DNA sequence is an impossible dream. Instead, it is a reality that will enable scientists to make many determinations and discoveries regarding the human, especially in the area of behaviour. It is evident that in the near future there will be a clearer understanding of answers regarding "nature vs. nurture" in terms of human capability and functioning.

In a paper written by BM Gupta and A Bala, named *Parkinsons's disease in India: An analysis of publications output during 2002-2011,* it is estimated that 6.3 million people suffer from PD worldwide. The World Health Organization gives an "estimated crude prevalence" (the total number of existent cases each year, old and new) of 160 per 100,000, and an estimated incidence (the number of new cases each year) of 16-19 per 100,000.

The Parsi community, in Mumbai, according to the researchers, has the world's highest incidences of PD where it affects about 328 out of every 100,000 people despite living in a country, India, with one of the world's lowest incidence of PD (70 out of 100,000).

The incidence of PD varies across the globe. However, this distribution may not be as simple as a geographical or ethnic factor. It is known that the PD is more prevalent in North America and Europe than in Asia and West Africa. However, research has been carried out to know the causes of PD and the use of medicinal plants for its treatment, prevention, and cure.

In China alone, says the paper, there are more than 1.7 million people with PD. The prevalence of PD per 100,000 of population varies from country to country, with highest in Albania (800) followed by Egypt (557), USA (329-107), Israel (256), Japan (193-76), Germany (183), Spain (170-122), Italy (168-104), Finland (166-120), Bulgaria (164-137), Estonia (152), Australia (146-104), England (139-121), Portugal (135), Cuba (135), Canada (125), China (119-57), Scotland (129), Norway (102), Thailand (95), Sweden (76), New Zealand (76), Nigeria (67), Poland (66), Jordan (59). Its prevalence, however, differs within countries.

The prevalence among Bulgarian Gypsies in only one-tenth of that found among Bulgarians. The prevalence in the USA tends to differ according to race, with Hispanics, then Whites, then Asians, then Blacks being more prone. The incident rate at which people with PD are newly diagnosed differs greatly according to the country.

The paper revealed that India ranks 16th among the top 20 most productive of research papers of countries with PD. And its global publications share of 1.47% during 2002-2011. The cumulative publications output of India in PD increased from 137 during 2002-2006 to 321 papers during 2007-2011, witnessing a growth of 134.31%

Despite the low prevalence of PD in India (except the high prevalence found in the small Parsi community in Mumbai), the country's research performance in this neurological disorder is quite good in the global context, says the paper. However, the country needs to intensify the quality and quantity of its research in PD carried out by different organizations including government institutions, government-supported research laboratories, and as a part of R and D programs of pharmaceutical industry with international collaboration.

Although millions are invested every year in the country in different areas of research, significant funds should be assigned for research in PD with proper supervision and clearly defined goals, say the researchers. To provide the comprehensive knowledge, information, and the best standard of care for this disorder, comprehensive management programs, various campaigns related to awareness, and education among people should be launched by the government. Besides this, innovative strategies and policies should be formulated to strengthen the neurological care within the existing health systems suggest the researchers.

WISH TO PUBLISH WITH US?

We are always keen to look at interesting content across genres. Please email your submission to: **submissions@leadstartcorp.com**

The submission should include the following:

1. **SYNOPSIS**
   A summary of the book in 500 - 1000 words. Please mention the word count of the manuscript.

2. **SAMPLE CHAPTERS / POETRY**
   A couple of chapters from the book; these need not be in order, just send the best two chapters of the book. Or a few poems if the same is a collection of poetry.

3. **A NOTE ABOUT THE AUTHOR**
   An interesting note about yourself (about 200 words).

4. **ADDITIONAL INFORMATION**
   - Target audience
   - Unique selling proposition
   - List of illustrative content (if any)
   - Other comparative titles
   - Your thoughts on marketing the book